Hell's Gate

By

Malcolm Hollingdrake

Dedicated to the memory of

Alan Doherty and Jack Dewar.

"The better I get to know men, the more I find myself loving dogs."

— Charles de Gaulle

Chapter One

The cold had a cruel habit of creeping slowly into his bones once he was tucked away from the dissipating day's heat. Even the new cardboard bedding he'd dragged in seemed suddenly damp. He twisted the cork from the bottle of cheap brandy and allowed the amber liquid to tumble to the back of his throat but even that failed to take away the insidious chill. At least he felt safe. This place was fairly secure and unaffected by the vagaries of the weather, although the constant, cutting draught that permeated through the grilled, yet open entrance seemed to constantly gnaw at him. He was, however, tucked well into the manhole that had been expertly crafted into the stone wall's façade and this was, for him, a psychological cocoon that he failed to find out on The Stray.

A small candle flickered weakly, illuminating dimly his grim surroundings. Bulging black bin bags of clothes were stuffed casually into the corners of his temporary accommodation. White needle-like stalactites hung from the brick, arched ceiling and the occasional flying bat distracted his eye. It was his fifth night in his new dwelling and he liked its darkness and security.

It had been a squeeze getting through the entrance bars. He had attempted entry on other occasions but the grids were too secure. However, this time they had seemed looser. Had he been capable, metaphorically, of reading the illegible graffiti on the wall, he might not have entered. He might have turned and found another shelter, but the dry, secure home, despite the constant sound of dripping water, was worth the trouble and the degree of risk. He looked at his shaking hand in the flickering, yellowy light; nails black and grimy. He had not always been this way, once he had had a family, a job, a home and a car but…the drink and the gambling had seen an end to such comforts. He could not now recall which hurdle had tripped him first and really he did not care. He took out his wallet, empty apart from three photographs. He looked at each in the dim flicker of candlelight and the images brought him a degree of warmth that was sadly tainted by the bitterness brought to the lump in his throat by his own selfish immaturity. He pulled the wallet to his chest and whispered the words, "Forgive me!"

It was the unexpected noise near the entrance that made the vagrant's heart beat more strongly and instinctively he blew out the candle. Hot, molten wax spilled onto his hand. The last thing he wanted was a gang of youths pissing about and tormenting him. He cocked his head and looked towards the echoing, alien sounds. Lights, thin white beams, danced around the arched roof like ancient searchlights, enlarging and deforming shadows and human features. He squashed himself tightly into the corner and prayed they would leave. His anxiety was real and suddenly he felt no cold, just the warmth of the fear he had so often experienced; he knew all about man's intolerance of man.

The human snuffling and snorting sounded more porcine than human, growing deeper as the youth was manhandled through the grid. Even though the youth was fully aware that his efforts were useless, vapour streamed from both his nostrils, his chest heaved as he squirmed and struggled. Tears had already begun to blur his vision and streams of snot dribbled onto the knotted cloth that filled his mouth, blocking breath and conscious sound alike.

Hands on the youth's shoulders forced him downward. The discarded garden seat on to which he was dragged was wet and cold against his naked buttocks, the steel frame rusty and rough against his sweating skin. His clothes had been discarded some time ago. Mud oozed between his toes and he could feel the sharp pain where broken glass and pieces of stone had punctured the soft soles of his feet. The people around him proved difficult to see; each wore a powerful head torch that created a contrast between blinding lights, silhouettes and shadows. Occasionally, when one head turned to the other, he identified the familiar faces of those surrounding him, once his friends. Large, electrical ties secured his elbows behind him, pushing out his chest pigeon-like. All seemed to grow quiet apart from the occasional plop of water hitting some distant, dark puddle but it was the next occurrence that the frightened youth could never have anticipated.

There seemed a moment of absolute silence where satanic forces grew more alive, co-operating fully with the present evil; even the falling droplets co-operated but the quiet was short lived. Hands forced the elastic band of a torch around his head holding it in position just above the eyebrows. The figure directly in front was handed a staple gun and immediately the sharp pain made his body twitch as the thin, metal staple penetrated the skin on his forehead and then splayed against his skull, trapping band to flesh. Blood trickled down his sweat-wet face and blended with the snail-path of snot, then another click of the gun, more pain and then another. Quickly the band was stitched to his head.

"We'll need to be able to see your progress, you shit! We'll need to see where you go and we don't want you to lose the light. The switch will be broken. There's only one way to run and that's what you do well, right little runaway? But you failed at that last time you were caught and brought home. This time you need to win or else…The way you run is that way. Get on top of the wall and you'll be safe, you'll be given another chance, just one more chance, but fail, and nobody will hear from you again."

The face moved closer and the garlic vapour, like a small cloud, filled his nostrils. It was pungent but somehow ridiculously reassuring that he had eaten the same meal. His mind spun, he recognised his error and his recklessness, definitely foolish and certainly inexcusable. Blood dripped onto his thigh before running down his leg to be diluted in the stinking mud. The penetrating beams of light hurt his eyes. It suddenly seemed that his senses had come alive and had increased ten fold, the pumping adrenalin and crippling fear had made sure of that.

"You get four minutes, four. Run fast and keep running. You really don't want what is behind you to find and catch you!"

The speaker spat directly into the captive's face.

"That's for your disrespect. You were treated like a son. It's now up to you, bastard."

The torch on his head was illuminated and the switch snapped off before the straps holding his arms were cut.

"Go!" they all screamed, the echo reverberating within the confined, black space.

After a brief pause, his heart racing and his pulse thumping in his ears, he started his slippery run, arms pumping, and eyes wide, into the chasm, into the unknown. Mud oozed between his toes as he moved over the parallel indentations running across the floor, making movement difficult. He just had to get away, he had to escape. He was unaware that an unknown, unsympathetic pair of eyes would briefly watch his progress.

"Run you little shit, run!" they all called, striking in him more fear and uncertainty of what was to come. Their sounds of laughter boomed as they bounced off the stonework

"Get them ready!"

Drew Sadler pushed himself as flat against the wall as possible, his breath instinctively held. Sweat now beaded his face as the heavy breathing and whimpering of the desperate youth grew louder as he approached. The cavernous space amplified the sounds that accompanied the naked figure running and stumbling past. Light beams danced on his back but it would be the next moment, the next split second that would bring the sudden and unexpected terror into Drew's private world.

Chapter Two

Rares Negrescu sat with his feet on the edge of the Formica-topped kitchen table. They formed a 'V' as he brought his toes apart before bringing them back together, deliberately blocking the view of the empty vodka bottle and Stella's tussled, blonde head. The snort from the end of the makeshift, rolled, paper straw that protruded from her left nostril could be heard even above the two growling, excited dogs in the next room. The thin line of white powder had disappeared, expertly vacuumed. He opened his feet. She looked up, wiping the end of her nose with her grubby, index finger before provocatively inserting it into her mouth. She looked directly at Rares, her suggestive finger slowly moving between her lips. The noise of the dogs increased and a child's scream made him close his eyes. Whatever idea Stella might have had of seduction it was neither subtle nor enticing enough to distract him from the chaos that was taking place in the next room.

"Fuck! If your brat is mauling with the pups again, I'll give her something to scream about!"

"It's them evil fuckin' dogs of yours, they shouldn't be with her."

"Fuck you!" he yelled, bringing his feet against the edge of the table kicking it into Stella's chest, causing the bottle to pirouette delicately before crashing, unbroken on the soiled floor.

The tone of the dogs changed. The scream intensified bringing shivers to Stella's body. Rares slid the bolt from the kitchen door and opened it. A large, growling Ridgeback burst through the gap, dragging Stella's brat by the head and shaking the child. A track of shiny, red trailed wet onto the dirty lino. The scream stopped. Attached to the child's badly deformed left leg was another Ridgeback, the bitch, who started pulling what looked like a saggy, rag doll in the opposite direction.

As one scream died, a second, deeper, more animal wail echoed round the tiled room. Rares lunged for the dog, grabbing it by the ear, shouting a command before biting it hard. The dark coloured hair, running along its back was standing proudly. The dog stopped, shook the child one more time, then dropped her. The over-excited bitch dragged what seemed like a lifeless body back through the door to where her five pups played excitedly, Rares followed.

Chapter Three

The broken storm clouds swam round the, grapefruit-coloured moon, blackening an imaginary eye. Chimneys of various sizes and dimensions poked skyward, belching out black, grey and white smoke, which leaned awkwardly at various angles depending on its density. Fiery light escaped from the silhouetted, factory windows, orange and yellow before reflecting and spreading on the wet pavements. No figures moved. Cyril studied the catalogue photograph of the painting with care. He pushed his frameless, reading glasses further onto his nose. He liked what he saw. He inhaled the menthol vapour from his electronic cigarette. A day off mid-week was a luxury but a necessity considering the hours Cyril had put in.

He loved the full auction experience from the moment a new catalogue arrived by post. He enjoyed the research, the copper in him was certainly in evidence, the study of the chosen artist, the viewing of a particular piece right through to the pulse-increasing anticipation of purchase. This would be accomplished, hopefully, at the lowest possible price. For Cyril, these were the elements that made up the heady, eager to swallow, art world cocktail. But it was not all plain sailing; he had been bitten on occasion, drawn along by other bidders, eventually paying over the odds. Generally, however, he had been lucky; he had now collected a small, but select group of paintings by Northern artists. If he had researched correctly, and bought wisely, the artwork would prove to be a reasonable investment. He had sold at auction, too, but that was a very different kettle of fish and was certainly not for the faint hearted, more of an extreme sport!

The main auction room was full, a vast collection of potential purchasers along with the objects to be purchased sharing the same space; a large hangar-type building that had little character and no acoustics. The day's auction seemed slow; Cyril inhaled more menthol nicotine vapour as he stood, immaculately dressed as always, looking towards the auctioneer's dais. To his left sat four people either ready to, or in the process of taking phone bids. Those punters making the effort to attend the auction had three invisible rivals, the phone bidder, the Internet bidder and those who simply left a commission bid.

Cyril looked at his watch and sighed. He shook his wrist before watching the second's hand sweep, smoothly round. He loved this watch, a present to himself for his fortieth birthday; he'd always wanted an Explorer 2 and decided if he could not treat himself at forty, then he would never invest in a Rolex.

Cyril stood to the side and glanced at the rows of bidders, each holding their specific bidder's number. He could never really fathom who might bid for what, but he could guarantee that somebody amongst them was about to bid on his chosen lot. There would certainly be someone ready with a phone or watching, hidden within the Internet. Lot 686 was shown on the large screen next to the auctioneer and Cyril's adrenaline level climbed along with his heart rate...

"Let the battle commence!" he whispered to himself as he stood more upright and leaned forward in anticipation.

"Lot 686 is this beautiful Theodore Major oil painting. Good provenance. You don't see these every day and sadly he's not painting any more... I have interest on the book. I have commission bids... and I can start straight in at... five thousand, five thousand five hundred. I welcome bids of six thousand pounds." The auctioneer smiled knowing it was going to be a strong lot.

Cyril was not surprised. He did not move but remained as calm as possible considering his heart jumped in anticipation and excitement. He stood now a little more nonchalantly, tucking his cigarette into his inside jacket pocket, not trying to signal that he was an eager buyer. A number of other regular bidders noticed his change of posture.

"Six five, thank you, seven, seven five to the Internet bidder."

Cyril lifted his catalogue and those who had taken notice, simply smiled. It was good to know your enemy. One of those watchers now raised his finger, only a small twitch, but the auctioneer spotted it straight away. A regular!

"Eight thousand pounds, new room bidder. Eight five now on the telephone,"

The auctioneer turned and looked at Cyril. Cyril nodded.

"Thank you, nine thousand pounds in the room, nine thousand to the gentleman here on my left. The auctioneer glanced at the other room bidder but received only a small shake of the head. I shall sell then, for nine thousand pounds. You are out on the phone and the Internet is quiet."

Cyril breathed deeply about to hold his bidder's number up victoriously. His estimate had been about right. The auctioneer raised his gavel whilst glancing at the computer screen.

"Nine five, new internet bid." He lifted his head. "Just in time!" His smile was not becoming!

The auctioneer turned to Cyril extending the gavel as if it were a begging bowl. "One more, Sir? Please, if you need, take a minute."

With a little hesitation Cyril held up his number, frightened that he was being caught in an auction moment of madness. He made a sign signalling to the auctioneer his intended bid, nine thousand seven hundred and fifty pounds.

"Thank you, yes that's fine, Sir. The next bid is ten thousand pounds," he announced with a knowing smile, trying to coax more from the bidders in the room, whilst anticipating another bid on the computer screen that did not materialise.

It had been Cyril's last bid. He was already seven hundred and fifty pounds above his planned expenditure but then it was a stunning painting, besides this was one reason he went to work every day and that, as well as being single, had to have some rewards. The sound of the crashing gavel stirred him.

"Nine thousand, seven hundred and fifty pounds, thank you, Sir."

The auctioneer smiled and nodded before noting Cyril's buyer's number.

Cyril could feel the perspiration, cold within his armpits and his mouth suddenly seemed dry. Spending was certainly hard graft. It was at this point within the process that uncertainty always seemed to creep in. The hammer price would probably come to thirteen thousand once the auction house and droit de suite costs had been added. Collecting his catalogue and his bidder's number, Cyril left the room.

He paid, collected his receipt and handed it to a porter. Within minutes the Major was in his hands. An immediate smile came to his lips. He turned to go when the other room bidder approached.

"Congratulations! That's a fine painting. You have a good eye." He smiled before glancing at the Major. "Well done. Good to see it sold to the room and not the bloody web!"

***

The drive back was uneventful apart from stopping in Masham for a swift celebratory half of Black Sheep Bitter. The rain mingled with the smell of hops that hung in the town from the two breweries, some would say like a bad smell but to others it was perfection. The rain grew stronger; it would be good to be home.

Robert Street, Harrogate, was quiet, apart from a large, articulated wagon performing an acrobatic, balletic, master-class in the art of blind reversing at the top of the street. The large supermarket deliveries had to be received in the bowels of the earth beneath the store. On numerous occasions during the week, the drivers had to reverse their containers across the main road, down the narrow slope and out of sight. To some it was second nature, to others it was probably their idea of hell. To the delayed motorists, waiting and watching, it was a pain in the arse!

Cyril's eye had been correct, the painting looked wonderful in the room. A small spotlight enhanced the orange of the factory lights; he could almost hear the cotton machines at work. "Has a look of Hades," he said out loud. He had just uttered the word 'Hades' when his phone rang. It startled him, moving magically on the table as it vibrated. Cyril's head dropped. He went to retrieve it.

"Bennett."

Chapter Four

The sound of the flock of sheep high on the Romanian hillside was carried on the light breeze. The air was fresh and the grass damp beneath bare feet. Wadim laughed as he dragged the homemade kite behind him. At first it clung to the green, coarse strands uncertain as to its true role in life but it soon bounced before beginning to claw at the invisible air. Slowly and less reluctantly, it lifted, higher and higher as the string was released through excited hands. The coloured tail of tied strips of magazine was whipped away by invisible hands that were trying to wrest it from flight as the small boy tugged, pulled, laughed and skipped. His eyes were focussed, constantly watching in astonishment at the successful first flight of his valuable, homemade toy. Now settled aloft, the kite floated, caressed by the breeze, almost in the hover. Only the tiniest end to the string remained in his fingers. The kite's painted face, now higher than Wadim could imagine, stared down at its eager, innocent, laughing creator who stared back with equal pleasure. Wadim could now rest and marvel. It was a good day and his usual pangs of hunger soon were lost with the increasing strength of the wind, the length of this maiden flight and the tugging of the string precariously gripped in his dirt-grained fingers. It was like the kite was alive!

The distant, approaching car crept into Wadim's peripheral vision, reluctantly drawing his attention and curiosity. He turned, glanced and then looked back at his beautiful kite. The sound of the motor now broke the silence, demanding Wadim take another look. He saw dust billowing from behind the off-white, battered 4x4 and he concentrated to see if he recognised the car. He knew it was a Lada, there were many but not as many as horse drawn carts in this area. He allowed it to distract him a little too much. The string slipped from his grasp, and the kite fluttered higher before being blown towards the copse of oak. He wanted to watch both the car and his kite; the kite won. He noticed it catch the upper branches of the tree before cascading from one branch to another, finally tangling within the thinner branches closer to the ground. With a little climbing which he assured himself he was good at, he was confident that he could retrieve it safely.

Once on the bough, he edged his way out, legs either side acting like a high wire walker's pole, his hands gripping in front. The kite dangled, pendulum-like as it swayed enticingly in the breeze. Tiny fingers stretched to reach the rough string but failed. A little further. His bare feet pushed against the bark and he felt the bough sag just a little as he moved along its diminishing girth. He tried again to reach, stretching his arm as far as he could. He was so close, but yet another move was needed. Pushing with his feet, he touched the string and made an eager grab. In his excitement he lost his one-handed grip of the bough. Desperately, he tried to hold on with only his thighs but this proved impossible; his legs swung left and then right trying to correct his loss of balance. The bark scratched and tore at the tender flesh of his inner thighs. As if by magic, the grass quickly exchanged places with the sky and he was falling, dragging the string and kite with him.

The sudden stop took away his breath and locked it somewhere in his chest where momentarily he could not find it. Gasping, gulping, panicking and unable to breathe; his body hurt, he felt nauseous. All went dark. The trickle of blood ran warm on his scratched legs. Sucking to get air, he opened his eyes and for a moment, the light calmed him but as quickly as the light had arrived, a shadow swiftly blocked out the sun's dappled rays. A large, silhouetted figure now confusingly covered his field of vision.

"Are you bene little fella? That was some fall." The stranger spoke gently before looking up at the bough and then at the kite in the gasping boy's hand. "What's your name and where's your ken, eh?"

Wadim knew the words, the Romany cant, they were all Roma living in and near his village of Ponorata. He certainly was not good and, yes he would like to go home but words did not want to come. They were locked with his strangled breath somewhere in his middle.

"What shall I call you?" The stranger bent down allowing the dappled light to stream back onto Wadim's face.

Between broken breaths he managed, "Wadim, Wadim Anghelescu... Is... my kite... broken?"

Large, smooth hands ran down his arms and legs. "Nothing broken, no bones and certainly not your kite, but some bad scratches on your legs and your kite's lost some of its tail. We've got ourselves one fallen, tough, little angel, Wadim Anghelescu. Unlike your kite you need more practice at flying, little man. Your kite is better at staying in the sky than you are staying in the tree." He smiled and moved Wadim's hair from his face.

Wadim, his breathing now more under control, allowed himself a smile. "Mother calls me her little angel... sometimes."

"Come on, I'll carry you to my car. Tell me if it hurts or are you just being brave?"

The stranger picked him up with care, watching the small face grimace with pain. A small tear appeared on the lower lid of one eye and rolled down his cheek.

"Keep your kite close. I'll take you to your ken in my car."

He lifted the boy, tilted the passenger seat with his arm and carefully placed him in the back seat before he climbed in. *If all his jobs were as easy as this, he'd be laughing*, he thought.

The car moved away quickly heading in the direction of Wadim's home and the boy began to relax. He studied his kite and his fingers caressed the frayed string where part of the colourful tail had once been tied. The car picked up speed, springs protesting at the uneven road surface. It turned sharply off the side-road and onto the main carriageway heading away from his promised destination. Wadim's heart gave a slight flutter as his eyes darted to the dark, dust-covered window. He knew this was wrong, the car was going too fast and he was heading towards town.

"Mister, you're going the wrong way!" His voice was high-pitched and frightened.

The driver turned and smiled, but said nothing.

Wadim tried to push the seat but it would not move. He started to scream and kick the back of the seat so hard he hurt his toes, before trying to climb into the front of the car. He grabbed the driver's hair who simply brought his hand from the wheel, turning it into a fist before he smashed it backwards into Wadim's forehead. The boy's body collapsed rag-like crashing into the back seat foot-well. Blood trickled from his nose. The kite flew briefly before it settled protectively on Wadim's shoulder.

Chapter Five

Although the new Harrogate Police Headquarters had a reputation for being extremely energy efficient, it also had the reputation for being a bit of a sieve. It was renowned for letting in water! From the early days, it had required strategic planning to place buckets in the correct position to catch the myriad droplets, but today, Cyril had noticed that the number of buckets needed to catch the water when it rained were now fewer. It seemed only when the rain was lashing from a certain direction did they need all of them. They needed none when it was fine unlike the first few months when water droplets had appeared when it was not raining. The experts believed it to be condensation caused through lack of adequate ventilation. Cyril often thought that the same architects who designed this building designed tower blocks and a shudder would run through him.

He moved towards his desk and instinctively straightened a few files and a variety of ornaments that had been disturbed by the cleaner. A shadow eclipsed the room and Cyril looked up. DS David Owen smiled, his huge frame blocking the door and the light. Cyril noticed that he held a cup and saucer in one hand and a mug in the other.

"Hope it's a clean cup, Owen," Cyril quizzed as he finished his domestic duties. "Thanks for the call. Good morning."

David Owen had always been known as Owen since his training days and that was how he was known in the department. He looked at Cyril, unsure if he were being facetious but he knew that if he had not called, there would have been hell to pay.

"Morning, Sir. Thought you might like a brew. Were you successful yesterday?" Owen really had little interest in art auctions or aesthetics but thought he had better ask.

"Bought a Theodore Major. Wonderful, Owen, simply wonderful. Great brush strokes and fantastic atmosphere."

Owen noticed Cyril's eyes glaze as if he were in love. "Major, Sir?" his tone, not too confident and containing a certain hint of confusion.

"And your day, Owen?" Cyril sipped his tea. "That's a good brew!"

"Football, Sir. Got to say if we coppers performed as badly as the players last night, the cells would be empty and the barristers would be cleaning windows. Not good, not good! Worst sporting spectacle I've ever seen. Waste of my time and my hard earned brass. The centre..." Owen looked up mid-sentence and paused, recognising from Cyril's facial expression that the centre forward's performance was of little interest to him. The conversation was over.

"The child, Owen, what've you got?"

"Mother's with the child. Her partner, Rares Negrescu is downstairs, dogs to be destroyed. There were two pups, they're with the RSPCA but there appears some doubt about the number in the litter. Can they destroy the pups for the sins of the parents? It was a bad one, Sir. Child amazingly survived but very badly mauled. We've had complaints from neighbours about the aggressive nature of the animals on five, separate occasions but no action was taken. Only recently can we take action if the dogs are not in a public place but nothing since that date. Mother's in a dreadful state, mind. As far as we know her partner's Romanian, been in the country three years, first Leeds, then Harrogate. We believe that he lives with her just off the Knaresborough Road, works at a Chinese kebab house on Shaw Street most evenings. No previous."

"A Chinese kebab house..." Cyril emphasised each syllable as if tasting the food. "What ever next will be added to our Yorkshire, culinary palate? So what was done about the complaints regarding the dogs? What about previous in his other life...Romania you said?"

"Ridgebacks aren't on the list of dangerous dogs so they don't need to be registered. Kept them mostly in the back garden and the complaints come from parents in the area. It seems strange too that there were no complaints of noise or barking. They report that the dogs appeared very aggressive when out with him, that they needed a great deal of restraint. Postman won't call either owing to some incident when they were not in the back. No bite, but a close thing. A Mrs Makin reported that they attacked her dog whilst on the lead and that they took some separating but he denied the incident. The postman incident was pre May, this year and before the amended Dangerous Dogs Act came into effect. Nothing yet about his past in Romania, Sir."

"So the law has been broken, dogs aggressive in a public place. Was he cautioned? Did someone at least visit?"

"Community Officer called and gave a warning. He saw a dog and it was neither aggressive nor out of control. He spoke with neighbours and they agreed that things had calmed down. Negrescu denied that his dog attacked another. The report also states he showed little understanding and apparently kept apologising for his limited knowledge of English. There may be resentment by the neighbours as the property is Housing Association and is situated within a row of private houses."

"Have you had the full medical report?"

"Not yet, Sir."

"Has this Stella got a surname?"

Owen perused his notes. "Gornall, Sir. Stella Felicity Gornall. Twenty-eight. Reverted to her maiden name last year. Married a Petev Costin, also Romanian, two years ago but his whereabouts are presently unknown."

"No doubt a marriage of convenience? Now probably swallowed in the system clawing benefits on false papers as well as sending child benefits home to the wife and five kids he has over there."

Owen simply raised his shoulders and pulled a face that suggested it might be so.

"I must be growing too old and too cynical. Blood tests on both adults?"

"They've come through; she's a drug user, showed signs of both cocaine and excessive alcohol in her system. He was clean."

Owen looked again, flicking the pages over trying to keep ahead of Cyril. He noted mentally that Social Services had not yet been involved.

"Caring mother!" whispered Cyril as he sipped the last of his tea. "He was clean I see. Are we sure neither drugs nor alcohol? I want to talk with him now, get DS Graydon to chat with the mother, take her under her wing. I hope..." He looked down briefly. "Negrescu has been cautioned and legal representation offered, yes? Do we have a translator?" He looked up over rimless glasses at Owen. "I also want an expert to look at the dogs."

Owen watched Cyril's right eyebrow lift independently. Often it occurred when he grew either more serious or more angry. It always seemed to bring to mind Gary Barlow of Take That. Whenever he introduced a song his right eyebrow had a similar uncontrolled life; it was as if it had a mind of its own.

"Translator, Owen. Yes or No?"

"On the way, Sir, sorry."

***

The man leaned back in the chair and simply stared at Cyril as he entered the room. He made no move to alter his position but simply chewed a fingernail before spitting it onto the floor. Cyril stopped, glanced at the Support Officer and nodded. As if by telepathy the officer moved towards the prisoner and brought him to his feet.

For a man who had been in the country three years, Rares Negrescu showed little inclination to use the language.

"Detective Chief Inspector Bennett. I'm sorry to hear about the child... if you fail to sit on the chair correctly it will be removed." Cyril's tone was forceful and he maintained full eye contact. "Understand? Now sit."

"Christina, is her name. Christina," Negrescu said without lifting his head. "My grandmother's name."

"I believe from this report that your partner left Christina alone for only minutes when the dogs attacked. Tell me again what happened."

Cyril sat back and studied the young man's facial features and his awkward body language but said nothing even though the pause brought an expanding void. Cyril noticed Negrescu looking up briefly and was immediately aware of not only arrogance but also coldness in his eyes. He also noticed the upper part of what appeared to be amateur tattoos on either side of his neck, mostly concealed by his collar.

"I told everything before. Nothing change. Her dogs." He looked down, moving forward placing his hands on the table leaning towards Cyril before locking eyes. "You kill her dogs, Policeman, yes? In my country, police cruel and unkind too."

Cyril held his stare longer than Negrescu anticipated he would. "Only when we have found all the information we can from them. How many pups?"

"Two."

"That too we shall verify. Amazing what our team can discover from both the living and the dead. We shall also be checking your place of work, your paperwork, your claims, your bank details, your family connections, your benefits and right at this moment we are searching your partner's home. Need I say any more?" Cyril didn't lift his eyes.

"I have told you, the stupid bitch allowed our child to be in the room. I thought Christina was in bed. I've told her over and over again when the pups are there she shouldn't let our child be alone. The dogs will protect their young. She knows that. Too much vodka. The dogs are hers but they are good, I only help with them. I have done nothing so you cannot keep me here... only twenty-four hours, I think."

"Let's hope Christina has twenty-four hours shall we? Thought you might like to know how she's getting on, foolish of me even to consider it." He removed his glasses. "Your English is better than you make out Mr. Negrescu. What else are you trying to hide?"

It was a rhetorical question. Cyril stood and made sure the chair scraped along the floor breaking the sudden silence. Cyril waited for Negrescu to look at him before he shook his head, smiled and lifted an eyebrow. "So where do you live? We know Stella lives in the Housing Association property, receives housing benefit or is it Universal Credit now? Available for a single mum living without a partner, because, Mr. Negrescu, she lives alone according to these records. So as I said, where do you live? Because if you live with her you have already broken the law... fraud, you understand, fraud?" He smiled again before turning to leave. "You have also contravened the Dangerous Dogs Act. I'm sure you are aware of the changes made this year. It's on your charge sheet. He was two up and he wanted Negrescu to understand that."

"Not my dogs, not my dogs," his voice growing more shrill.

Maybe Cyril was only one up.

Owen was waiting by Cyril's office.

"Stubborn, secretive, cowardly. Blames Stella, her child, her dogs. He'd warned her. He's as guilty as sin. He says the child was left for a few minutes. Yes... right! Mother's guilty he says, not the dogs' fault. Rubbish!" Cyril slapped the file with the flat of his hand. "Any news about the home?"

"Wouldn't exactly call it that, Sir. It's in a reasonable area. Very few homely comforts other than a big, flat screen TV and some second hand furniture. One room, the largest, seemed to be kitted out as a kennel. Good one too, that's where the priorities were. Child's room comprised little, a tiny cot, few toys and a black tarpaulin for curtains. Place could be technically classed as a *shit 'oyl* as my father would say! Forensics will be going through it. Interestingly too, there was little food in the house but there was quality dog food, lots of it."

Cyril lifted his eyebrow. "You're not suggesting..."

Owen simply shrugged his shoulders. "Medical report on the child will be here this afternoon, including photographs of her injuries. I've drafted this press release." Owen slipped it onto Cyril's desk. "There's a request for bail. If Stella Gornall did place the child in harm's way, against her partner's warning, even if he were a guest in the house, then who should be here? Drug user and under the influence of alcohol or…?"

"Owen, whose dogs? Why were they there? Why all the food and the front room kennel? If the child dies one is going to prison for longer than he or she would last year. Thankfully, the suspended sentences given out for fatal dog attacks are a thing of the past. Let's hope Christina pulls through."

Owen could sense real concern, an emotion he had seldom seen in his boss.

"Is Liz still with the mother?"

Owen nodded the affirmative. "Social Services are liaising with Liz and the medics. Child Protection will probably ensure that Christina remains in hospital until investigations can decide a safe way to progress…that too can be a can of worms."

"I want to see Liz as soon as."

"He walks at the moment but we need to know his address."

Liz knocked at the door and showed her face. "Sir, Owen." She nodded at them both. "Christina will be in hospital for some time. She'll need one or two more ops to sort out the facial wounds but she'll neither lose the leg nor is there any brain injury. Considering the two dogs, she's been a lucky little girl. There's been a strategy discussion and we're applying for an Emergency Protection Order. If it's successful, and there's no reason to believe otherwise, this will give us eight days with the possibility of increasing it a further seven after that to apply for a Supervision Order. I'll be attending. I want to watch out for this little lady."

Cyril smiled.

Chapter Six

The small French hotel nestled on the village street, two buildings separated by a car park. The old hotel had been recently modernised and the house next door converted into accommodation. It attracted people who were visiting the graves of those who perished in the Great War. It was a regular stopping place for Hai Yau.

Three cars were parked shrouded by morning condensation, their windows opaque and their paintwork matt. One was registered in France, one England and the other Romania. Hai Yau sat at the breakfast table beneath the stuffed head of a wild boar and talked constantly into the screen of an iPad. He spoke without pause and without facial expression, his nose almost touching the screen until a couple came into the dining room and he nodded a polite greeting. Hai Yau's wife, much younger than he, moved food around her plate, occasionally putting small morsels into her mouth. She turned and smiled at the couple before checking her mobile phone. Conversation over, Hai Yau moved back his chair and then walked out of the dining room.

Within a month his fourth restaurant in the UK would open and he would be developing some of his extra curricular business interests with it; this latest news he had just received displeased him, could he trust nobody to do the simple tasks?

***

Hai Yau removed his wallet and paid the hotel bill in cash. He neither spoke French nor made any attempt to; he bowed automatically and thanked the owner as he took the receipt and placed it in his wallet. He paused, eyes down, as he looked at the photograph of the boy who stared back proudly leaning on the roof of a small, yellow sports car. Hai Yau ran his thumb over the protective plastic, lifted the wallet to his lips and kissed the photograph.

"My son," he said proudly showing the hotel owner.

***

Hai Yau had lived in Romania since 1991. He remembered that his first impression of the country was a poor one but then all ports seemed the same, just the flags, flavours and smells differed. When you had spent years at sea there came a time to settle down and Hai Yau found Romania, a country just released from the communist grip, ripe for change. As the cook on The Albion, a merchantman registered in Panama, he was well liked and a few of the crew who were Romanian suggested he could do worse than open a Chinese restaurant. Times were changing and horizons were broadening in their homeland.

Although his first months proved difficult, his comparative wealth bought him a young Romanian bride, a restaurant in Constanța and a growing respect amongst the local business community. He employed his own, bringing people from his hometown, Wenzhou; they in turn brought skills and protection, a vital commodity. After three years he had four small restaurants and an even smaller protection racket. But one thing was missing, he had failed to father a child. That problem was soon solved as all problems could be providing the right people were contacted and the correct amount of money changed hands.

***

How the time had flown by since his little miracle, his angel had arrived. Now he was a vital pin in the machine. He closed the wallet. As a parting gift, the owner handed Hai Yau two bottles of wine. By tomorrow he would be home in Romania, others would be looking after the Yorkshire business.

Chapter Seven

Wadim's head hurt, it throbbed as he tried to focus. When he moved, the grazed flesh on his inner thigh made him whimper. He wanted to shout for his mum but something inside told him to be silent. Shutters blocked the light but he could just see the sky through a small crack from where he was lying. He moved quietly and put his eye to the gap before stepping back amazed at what he saw. Huge mansions were squashed together and painted in bright colours, each very individual, every one a small, architectural monstrosity. He had never seen anything like this and he was certainly not near home. He felt tears appear in his eyes and he began to sob as his thoughts drifted to his family and his home.

The door opened and light flooded the room. The stranger, who had originally seemed so kind, but then had hurt him appeared and Wadim screamed, running to the furthest corner.

"Brought you a friend, little Angel and I'll be bringing you food later." The man put the dog on the floor. "His name is Lupei and he'll look after you."

The dog, tail wagging, crossed the room and began to lick Wadim's legs. It tickled. He moved his feet in a half-hearted gesture to move the dog away but soon bent to stroke it. Lupei jumped to lick his face as if trying to take away the tears. The man gripped Wadim's cheek and squeezed before twisting. "He'll look after you."

He let go. Wadim rubbed his cheek, he hated that gesture and he told himself that he would not let it happen again. He looked down at the dog.

"You're not like a wolf as your name suggests."

At this, the dog rolled over and Wadim giggled, tickling its soft under-belly. A few minutes later the door opened again and a young woman entered carrying two bowls. In the half light Wadim could see her smile and he responded. She was no more than sixteen. Lupei stood and moved between Wadim's legs and he felt the dog stiffen as if on guard, bringing a rush of fear to Wadim's stomach.

"Are you protecting Wadim, Lupei?"

The dog growled and gave a short, sharp bark.

"Good, then this is yours." She put the bowl of food down in front of the dog. "Wait!" The dog sat and did as it was told.

"This is for you little Wadim, you must be so hungry."

Wadim could smell the stew and he could now see the steam rising from it. He could almost taste the large chunk of bread that nestled on the edge of the bowl as his mouth began to water. He took the proffered bowl with both hands.

"Here's a spoon. Enjoy it! Don't give any to Lupei otherwise he'll be your friend for ever." She smiled and winked. "Let's have some light in here."

Although the light stung his eyes it was good to see the room and the dog. Saliva dribbled from its chops as it stared at the food in front of it.

"When you start eating you can tell Lupei to eat too but only after you have eaten some of yours."

She left and closed the door. The lock turned. Wadim was already eating. The dog turned, eyes pleading, saliva splashing Wadim's legs.

"Mânca!" sprayed Wadim as his packed mouth articulated the short word. Food shrapnel splatted the dog's ear as it dived at the bowl. Neither took his time over the food but the dog won the race to finish and then turned to Wadim, eyes beseeching. It was a difficult decision but the dog won for the second time as the final morsels of food were tipped into its bowl. It was an easy decision, Wadim needed all the friends he could get. He also needed a toilet.

The door opened again and the woman entered carrying a bowl of water and a mug.

"That didn't take you too long. Drink this."

Wadim informed her that he needed the toilet. She took his hand and led him down some marble stairs, across the hallway and through into a large yard. Lupei followed. At the bottom of the yard was a shed, the toilet. The dog ran ahead before cocking a leg and spraying the corrugated shed wall. No matter how grand the house, the more traditional Roma do not use the toilet and cook under the same roof.

"Lupei was desperate too," she giggled. The door was pushed open, Wadim entered and the door closed.

"I'll be here."

The smell was overpowering and the light dim. Wadim emptied his bladder. The door opened and he took the girl's hand. He looked up at her and she smiled.

"Don't forget your drink, it should be still warm."

Wadim drank quickly and within minutes felt tired and a little dizzy. He lay on the bed and Lupei curled at his feet. He would not stir for a number of hours by which time he would be well on his way to his new home.

Chapter Eight

Three reports hit Cyril's desk within the hour. The first confirmed that the child would live. The photographs proved distressing but Cyril was amazed that she was not as badly injured as had first been thought. The second report regarding the dogs contradicted Negrescu's statement, there were more than two pups. Both adult dogs had been destroyed; the two pups were being looked after. The third file confirmed his guess that Negrescu had other accommodation albeit a mobile home, very Romany.

Owen knocked at the open door.

"Have you read these?"

Owen nodded. He reached into his back pocket and removed a rather crumpled five-pound note and handed it to Cyril who held it between thumb and forefinger before inspecting it as if it were a soiled handkerchief.

"Has it lived in there a while?"

"Since I last had this suit cleaned. How did you guess he was a caravan dweller?"

Cyril just tapped his stomach. "The wisdom of age, Owen. One day it will come to you."

The phone rang and Cyril answered. "Bennett." He said nothing else but put down the phone, closed the files and dropped them into the top, left hand drawer.

"Come with me Owen...no peace for the wicked and that statement clearly suggests you!" He smiled, more in disappointment than pleasure, took one inhalation from his electronic cigarette before marching through the door.

"Close it behind you, we'll be a while."

Owen let the door slam.

As they drove down Pannal Road, Owen could see the familiar tape and white-clad team and stopped by the police car that straddled the road. An officer approached and Cyril showed his ID.

"A motorist had a puncture and stopped, lucky really, chance in a million of finding this lot. It could have been here weeks if he'd not stopped."

It was true that the road was busy and the litter was only collected rarely.

"Hope you advised the guy not to do the lottery if stopping and finding a corpse is considered luck," Owen said to the officer and smiled.

"Things today, for the poor guy, can only get better unless you believe that mishaps always come in threes, Sir."

"Got all his details?" The officer handed his notebook and Owen copied the information. "We'll talk with the motorist later. How is he?"

"Shaken, very, very shaken. It's not pretty."

The body or body parts seemed to be strewn over a fairly wide area as if they had been discarded from a vehicle and it did not really take a trained eye to realise that it had either been butchered or torn apart. The SOCO team was busy taking photographs, measurements and samples. One of the attending officers moved towards Cyril.

"Real mess, Sir. Definitely white male, naked. Main torso is here."

A finger pointed to what looked like part of a dressmaker's mannequin, prostrate in long grass. "And various limbs are spread along the verge, mostly just over the hedge, no fingers and only parts of hands. The genitals have gone but that may be the result of foxes after the parts were dumped. We'll know when they were dumped after the pathologist, whose sampling now, has some results."

"What's all the rest of the stuff? Is it his clothing?" Cyril stared and pointed at various objects that were spread over a wide area.

"Looks at first inspection like they are just bags of clothing."

"Could this chap have been hit by a fast moving vehicle and then been dragged along causing massive injuries?"

Cyril did not seem to believe his own theory and his uncertainty was reflected in the question. Cyril recognised the Police Pathologist.

"We'll wait." He knew better than to interrupt her work at this stage of the initial inspection.

How anyone could refer to the mass of tangled pieces as he amazed him. There was not even a face as far as he could see and determining the sex, well, from what he could see he would not have liked a wager.

Cyril opened the car door and sat, his feet on the road, head down. He began to vape, the menthol infusion tickling the back of his throat. Owen leaned on the wing and twiddled with his phone. Cyril looked up and smiled as Owen's fingers danced on the small keypad.

"Your thumbs will be knackered by the time you're forty. Just put a call in for Traffic to be vigilant in all areas. We may be searching for a vehicle with excessive front-end collision damage. Probably a stab in the dark but then…"

Owen finished his text, changed phones and made the call.

The pathologist approached Cyril's car.

"Still taking unknown substances into the body, 'Flash'?"

Cyril smiled without looking up. He had collected the nickname early on in his career. Many believed it was because of his immaculate dress sense and keen eye for detail; they were wrong. Bennett was nicknamed *Gordon* originally after James Gordon Bennett, a very wealthy individual, promoter and patron of sports, especially those requiring impressive and expensive equipment. One such sport was motor racing and one of his main sponsorships was notably the Isle of Man Bennett Trophy races of 1900 to 1905. The TT races carry the name today. It was then that *Gordon* was linked with *Flash Gordon* after some drinking session in his early years and from then he was known as *Flash*. He still seemed to carry the moniker with him. It caused him little concern, however, as only certain individuals were brave enough to say it to his face.

Cyril looked up and offered her his hand. "Not heard that for a while." He held up the cigarette. "Only minty vapour, none of that bad stuff, oh and not forgetting the occasional pint of Black Sheep when work and the gym permits. Drawn the short straw Julie? Bit of a jig-saw this one!" Cyril smiled.

Dr Julie Pritchett was one of four Home Office Pathologists working in the North East and had known Cyril for some time.

She removed the paper suit and blue shoe covers, stuffing them into a plastic, yellow bag along with her gloves and facemask.

"Always the lucky one. Your case?"

Cyril nodded. "ALWAYS the lucky one Julie," he repeated and she detected a degree of fatigue. "You've met? ...DS Owen, known as Owen."

They shook hands.

"Well, he's been dead approximately four days give or take and not killed here. Body looks to have been washed down, smells like strong bleach so we'll not anticipate DNA contamination. Interestingly, we've spotted a small tattoo on his right cheek but we'll get clear images when he's back at the lab. Quite a large proportion of, shall we say, the smaller body parts are missing so it would be worth a search both ways along the length of this road. A finger would be most helpful."

Julie smiled and walked towards her car.

"Will ring when everything is in the lab. By the way that's a paradox."

Cyril looked puzzled. Julie started the car and drove towards Cyril before pulling up next to him. She lowered the window. "Gym and beer." She shook her head and smiled. "I'll be in touch."

Owen noted that the Crime Scene Manager was already organising a close area linear search to occur as soon as the body parts and various bags of detritus had been photographed, catalogued and removed. He was conscious of the time scale and he wanted it done as soon as possible. Pannal Road could not be closed off indefinitely. Before he had finished the call, the first specialist dog team had arrived but it would be a while before all the Forensic team had finished. Cyril just looked and smiled before mouthing, "Well done!"

Cyril would start handing over the completed reports, which would then be logged into HOLMES, the Home Office Large Major Enquiry System. Each would be allocated a unique message number opening a line of enquiry. The more details added would mean that clues or coincidences would not be overlooked.

***

On the opposite side of his office, two charging batteries for his electronic cigarette dangled listlessly from the plug sockets like small, cylindrical rodents. Each sported one glowing red light-like eye indicating it was low on energy. Sitting temptingly on a small plate was a large pork pie and three pickled onions. Cyril pushed at the pie with a knife and fork considering the number of calories it held. His will power was fighting a significant battle against his grumbling stomach. He knew that his waistline had increased steadily over the last year and he had, for the first time in his life, started going to the gym. He should eat only half, he thought, before he continued to maul it like a cat with a portly mouse. He ate the onions. His mobile phone rang and he could see it was Owen. He picked up the plate, tipped the pie into the bin and decision made, answered the call.

"Bennett."

"The dog has located what might be the part of a hand much further away from the rest of the pieces. It's going to the lab but it seems there's nothing else here. We'll do one more sweep and then open the road."

"Keep the roadside area taped and coned and have a patrol car on either side to keep the press and the public away. Any damaged vehicle reports?"

Cyril leaned over and looked at the pie in the bin. He could feel his mouth salivate. His stomach rumbled as if protesting over his rash decision. He needed a coffee.

"A local bus but the destroyed bollard speaks for itself. Will keep you updated. I'm releasing a press statement in an hour and that might harvest some witnesses."

The press release hit the local television and radio stations that afternoon and in turn filtered to social media. It gave a brief report of finding a male body and asked for anyone who had been in the area to report anything suspicious. To Owen's surprise there was an immediate response from a female taxi driver who had been travelling home at 01:30 the previous night. She had noticed a flatbacked truck stopped on Pannal Road.

"She's coming in this evening, she's a…" He looked at his notes. "Vicky Hutler." Owen stumbled over the last name.

Cyril turned and looked inquisitively at Owen. "Hutler or Hitler?"

"Says here…" Owen lifted the paper and looked with great care, "Hutler, Sir." He spelled out the name. "Here in about half an hour."

"Hungry, Owen?" Cyril knew better than to ask. "Had you been back earlier there was an Appleton's pork pie begging to be eaten but…"

"Enjoy it, Sir?" Owen's voice and facial expression showed his disappointment.

"In the bin. I was tempted but I'd rather miss half a gym session than consume unnecessary calories. In the bin." Cyril pointed feeling very self-righteous and was naïvely surprised by the response.

Owen moved to the bin and looked in. Cyril's bin was always empty and Owen bent and picked up the pie. He turned it through three hundred and sixty degrees inspecting it. A small piece of fluff was removed before he took a bite.

He looked at Cyril and smiled, his mouth full of pie. "Do you mind? My mum's always saying, *waste not, want not.*" Small pieces of crust cascaded from his lips landing on Cyril's desk.

"And mine said that there's nothing wasted where you keep a pig." He took a tissue from the box and wiped away the projectile detritus.

Owen looked affronted and lowered the pie, wiping his mouth on the back of his hand. Cyril took another tissue and handed it to Owen.

"Owen, I was joking for Christ's sake, just enjoy it, you've a bigger frame to fi…." He then stopped himself mid sentence realising that he was digging himself into a deeper hole.

***

The interview lounge was designed to be less intimidating than the standard, naked interview space, a more open room; pictures on the walls, a Yucca plant in the corner made for a more relaxed ambience. Vicky was sitting nursing a cup of coffee when Cyril and Owen entered. A WPC to her left would stay throughout the interview.

After introductions, Cyril explained to Vicky that the interview would be videoed and she was given a small booklet on her rights as far as data protection was concerned.

"As I said before, I was going home. I finish at 1am and as I travelled down Pannal Road there was a truck parked at the side of the road. A man was standing by the open driver's door, he waved me past, and another man was on the grass verge. I thought they were Council workers. The amber flashing roof lights were on and so were the hazard lights so it was easy to spot." Vicky drank more coffee.

"The men, did you notice anything unusual?"

"No. Yellow fluorescent jackets, hats and gloves. Nothing out of the ordinary, as I said. One waved me by after checking up the road; they looked as though they were inspecting the area. I've a forward in-car camera but it's been playing up. Sometimes it comes on with the ignition and other times it doesn't, seems to have a mind of its bloody own. I checked it but I only have the view into the car. Keeps a watch on passengers. You can never be too careful."

"Could you give a description of either person you saw?"

Vicky thought briefly and shook her head. "It was dark and I was tired. Long day!"

Owen leaned towards her. "Any chance we could borrow your camera? One of our technical lads might be able to sort it for you."

"No probs, brilliant, do you want it now?"

Vicky left after handing over the camera and Owen smiled. "If she passed the truck it might show through the rear window and our lads should be able to enhance the images. Who knows what they might find on the disc."

Cyril and technology did not make good bedfellows. "I'll leave you with your devil's work. I take it we didn't have a Council van or truck out on that stretch between 1 and 2am?"

Owen just shook his head.

"Thought not."

Cyril left.

Chapter Nine

Angel walked towards the prefabricated cabin that was positioned to the left of the farmyard. Wires protruded from the lip below the flat roof and linked to the stone wall like limp umbilical cords. He mounted the two steps and entered. A single strip light illuminated the space providing a harsh light; a Formica table and a chair added to the lack of ambience. The single window was boarded with plywood and a photograph of a semi-clad girl curled at the corner as if protecting her modesty. Angel turned to look at Rares who sat bolt upright, his face flushed. The snake tattoo that started behind one ear and finished behind the other was lost in his bright, red skin. A young man stood to either side, one hand securely resting on each of Rares' shoulders; he was going nowhere. Angel paced the single room, initially ignoring the occupants but since his arrival the atmosphere had grown far more claustrophobic.

"What the fuck happened? We lose two dogs and two pups as well as a safe house all because you cannot control your fucking woman's habit! The police are all over that place as if we didn't have enough to worry about. My father, believe me, is not happy with you and I guess you know the implications? It could cause you much pain, my friend, much pain."

Angel moved towards Rares and nipped his cheek before twisting his hand. Rares squealed as the twist was increased. "You know what this business is about, that we need to keep things calm and smooth."

From the timid boy who had chased his kite without a care in the world apart from the pangs of hunger, he had been moulded and formed into a strong, brutal young man, so much so, his nickname,

Angel, had stuck and the name Wadim had been surrendered to the mists of time. Father and son had bonded beautifully.

"The Police have already visited the kebab shop and you can thank my father that all your tax and employment affairs are in order. You were told to kennel the dogs with her, not live, not co-habit. You knew that! The child is not yours, you know that too." He struck Rares in the chest. "In here you know Christina is not yours. Stella gets paid for her services. It's part of the business. If they get a whiff that she has a partner who co-habits then they'll snoop and discover her other skills. She loses those benefits, we lose or should I say you'd lose. You know The Chase? You'd be the one in The Darkie."

One of the two young men lifted his hand to the red marks around his forehead and shivered as Rares nodded frantically, his eyes wide with fear and the pain in his cheek.

"Our animals are getting more hungry and more fierce. They are silent. They'll catch you quietly, all you'll hear is heavy, excited breathing getting closer and closer. They are, my friend, harbingers of great pain, suffering and eventually a very slow death. You know that, you make them so, they are your babies whereas Christina is not."

Angel released his grip on Rares' cheek and the mark was angry and red.

"One more chance for your freedom is more than most would get. We've already had one lucky bastard." He looked at the young man who was rubbing his forehead.

Both hands lifted from Rares' shoulders in unison and Angel left the room. The two sentries stayed with Rares and they immediately relaxed a little before the door opened and Angel re-entered with another man.

"You'll listen and listen good." Angel looked Rares straight in the eyes. "This man's here to tell you what you're to expect and what you have to do."

The stranger, dressed in a smart suit, was in total contrast to the others. He put a small case on the table and leaned on it before addressing the attentive audience in their native tongue.

"The police will be watching you from now on so you demonstrate how much you care about Christina. You visit, if allowed. I doubt that's possible but you try. If you go by the law and say you lived there before the incident, then you can see her but you open up a can of worms regarding Stella's benefits. You make polite enquiries at the hospital, that's all. No fuss, nothing. You work at the kebab shop and you go home. A routine. You don't change it. You don't come here until you're brought. You might find Christina's put in the care of a foster mother, which is normal under the circumstances. You mustn't try to find her if that's the case, the foster carer will not tolerate any interference. Are you listening?"

Rares nodded. The other two also nodded and Angel smiled inside.

"If we feel at any time that you're a threat to Mr Yau…" There was a pause that said more than a thousand words. "Well, I'll say nothing further. You all know the consequences, we are family and we stick together, no one leaves."

Angel now spoke quietly and put a gentle hand on Rares' shoulder. "Now go, the dogs in the barn need you. When your work with them is done you go back to your trailer."

Rares stood and thanked everyone, he was not sure why but it felt natural and as he left he thanked them again as he closed the door. The cool air brought relief from the pressure cooker he had just experienced.

"When he's done the dogs, take him back. Don't take him to his trailer, drop him within walking distance and do not use the truck, that remains secure until we learn what the police know." The two simply nodded.

Angel crossed the yard and entered the stone farmhouse. His father had bought it with certain criteria in mind, the first being seclusion, the second his need for multiple outbuildings and the third, just enough land and woodland to offer total privacy. The barns, apart from one set to the south of the farmhouse, had been converted into temporary accommodation for the people who were working within his various business interests. Each person was given an initial six-month work placement and after that, depending on their ability and fortitude, they either stayed or were moved on, a profitable enterprise.

With the opening of the new restaurant, another nine Romanian men and women were to be collected from the streets of major cities and towns, trained and given employment. Papers would be checked and if necessary created. Some migrants had a more natural ability than others. It all added to the positive statistics the Government wished to project, people were off the street and in work. After an induction, they would be moved away from the farm and if all went well, into houses and flats paid for with legitimate benefits. Hai Yau had the necessary staff to process claims and at the same time keep the claimants employed whilst relieving them of a large percentage of their benefit. Once they were in the system they would remain. Their passports were held and their freedom curtailed. Rumour and stories were enough to control most of them. Occasionally, only occasionally, they experienced a runner but the response and photographs of the outcome were enough to deter others. Besides, once trapped in the system, the workers quickly realised that they could trust no one. However, for many, this was still an improvement on their living standards back in Romania and many were now able to send money home. Each was encouraged to watch and listen. Rewards were offered for any information that might suggest someone was not happy with his lot. You did not leave voluntarily and you certainly did not run. Hai Yau and Angel, however, were not totally without heart. Some, once trusted, were allowed to return home for a short holiday to see family and friends but they knew that Hai Yau's tentacles were both cruel and long and only occasionally did one not return.

A large mesh fence had been secured around the perimeter of the farm and hung with signs warning that dogs were always loose. It kept away ramblers and nosey parkers.

Chapter 10

Cyril hated every moment of the gym session. He had organised six sessions with a personal trainer. Initially he had been extremely enthusiastic, eager to achieve his targets. His initial weight of 88kg was the heaviest he had been for as long as he cared to remember and what with his Doctor's talk of body mass index and obesity often in the news, he had realised it was one area of his life that he had allowed to run off track. Cyril liked order, cleanliness and rigor, above all else, rigor ran his life. Did the PT have to be so pushy and equally so demanding? He could appreciate why, the results were showing and after four full weeks he was a respectable 85kg. His target was 78kg and he would have to confess that he felt a good deal better.

The last of the spin session nearly proved to be the straw that broke the camel's back. He began to hate the man who made such heavy demands on him. Dripping with sweat, Cyril sat back and sipped water. To his surprise he felt refreshed and strangely invigorated. After showering he caught himself stealing a furtive, sideways glance at his own naked body. It was reshaping and he was thrilled; he still breathed in a little though, he noticed and smiled, unembarrassed by his vanity. It was ever thus!

Once home he cooked an omelette and ate before staring at the Major. "Just above Hades," he said to himself as he looked more deeply at the dark, smoking mills and the reflected orangey-yellow light. "No wonder later in his career Theodore Major became obsessed with skeletons and devils."

***

It was 7am when Cyril locked the front door of his stone, Victorian terraced home and turned left down Robert Street through the snicket onto West Park before crossing The Stray; two hundred acres of open grassland, to Cyril the lungs of Harrogate. He turned up the collar of his black, quilted coat against the cold and set his usual morning course for work. He loved this time, it gave him space to think, to put things in perspective in readiness for the day. He mentally prioritised and compartmentalised his thoughts so that by the time he had arrived at his office and made a brew, he would be up and running. He took his electronic cigarette from his pocket and inhaled the minty flavour. It gave him an inner sense of pleasure.

The traffic on Otley Road was busy but apart from stopping to buy a paper he strode out, all part of his exercise regime. *The Beehive* pub in which he had occasionally enjoyed a pint, had closed months earlier and was now going through the final stages of renovation. Cyril had been intrigued to watch its metamorphosis over the weeks. Smart, modern grey window frames and doors had been fitted and he admitted to himself that they complemented the building's stone façade. A new sign showed that it was going to be an Italian Restaurant, *Zingaro*. When it opens, he thought, he would give it a try and maybe even bring Julie. His mind butterflied to her and he visualised her trim figure moving to her car. A sharp blast from a car's horn brought him up swiftly as he had inadvertently stepped onto one of the many side roads that crossed his route. The driver, obviously angry and frustrated by the morning traffic, shook his head and put a finger to his eyes. Cyril got the connection and mouthed, 'Sorry'.

Owen watched his boss move to his desk and place the cup and saucer onto the mat before hanging up his coat. He followed him in with a perfunctory tap on the door.

"Morning, Sir. The guys had a look at the video camera and although there was nothing from the front we have these images from the rear."

Owen pointed to the laptop and held up the disc. Cyril sipped his tea and gestured for Owen to show him. The images were better than either had expected. They clearly showed the vehicle as the taxi passed and the driver moving to the rear of the truck. Owen announced that it was an Iveco that appeared to have had a hard life. He ran it again and stopped the film at a point where the driver was looking straight at the back of the taxi. Cyril put his cup down and slipped on his glasses before moving closer to the screen.

"What on earth is he wearing?" Cyril tipped his head to one side as if to get a better view.

"We were confused too, but on closer inspection it's a skull bandana worn over the mouth and nose, usually by skiers or motor-cyclists."

Owen's fingers tapped the keyboard and a complete collection of these morbid items came up from bandanas to full skull balaclavas.

"It's a bandana as they're easy to pull down and re-cover. It looks like the people we need to find."

Owen started the film again. "You'll see, there's no number plate nor reflection from one."

"Has anyone else come forward?"

Owen shook his head.

"Don't give any details to the press that we're looking for a truck or it will be a pile of ash and twisted metal by tonight. We should receive some lab results today."

"There's some good news, Sir."

Cyril just raised an eye-brow and took another sip.

"The technical lads have fixed her camera!"

Cyril simply raised both eyebrows and sighed. "I'm glad we're good at some things, Owen."

***

Cyril stood and looked at the variety of intriguing ornaments that were displayed on the glass shelf in Dr Pritchett's office. He was tempted to draw a smiley face in the dust but restrained the urge. He was sure the ornaments all came from some part of the human anatomy but he was not sure which part. The door opened and Cyril turned and smiled quizzically whilst pointing at some semi-spherical objects slightly smaller than cricket balls.

"Morning Cyril. Kidney stones believe it or not. It's amazing what the body will produce. Speaking of body and producing, that was a mess you discovered. Coffee?"

Cyril settled with a coffee and produced a small Dictaphone. "Do you mind?"

Julie shook her head.

"You were saying?"

"Male. Cause of death, heart failure brought about through severe body trauma. Attacked by dogs that were out of anyone's control. Not only attacked but also a good deal of body tissue was consumed, hence the missing fingers and facial features. We presume the dogs were starved. It could have been a pack but I doubt that. When was the last time you saw a stray on The Stray?" She grimaced at her own pun. "Let alone a pack of strays? The partial hand found later was, we believe, moved post mortem, probably by a fox, but the bleach used to clean the corpse would dissuade consumption. The scene of death must have been awash with his DNA. Considering the severity of the injuries, he probably bled out where he was attacked. Any ideas?"

Cyril shook his head.

"Clear traces of drug and alcohol abuse and marks of scabies and lice infestation, common with those that fall from grace and live rough."

"Any information from his dental records?"

"They're being scanned at present and we have photographs of the tattoo I mentioned to you at the scene. It appears to depict some cartoon character but there's damage. I thought it was Snoopy. The words, 'The Mad Punter' were discernable with some difficulty below it and that made me doubt my initial thought but my assistant agrees. It's forwarded for your attention."

The conversation was interrupted as a colleague entered and a sheet of paper was placed on the desk. Julie read it.

"Your man is a Mr Drew Sadler, 46. He's been living rough for the past twelve months or so and according to his records he's a divorced father of two. And to think that most people think their teeth are used only for chewing! His previous address is here along with a brief history. You owe me dinner." She smiled and handed Cyril the paper.

Cyril read through it again before folding it and putting it in his inside pocket. He switched off the Dictaphone.

"The dinner is off the record." She smiled.

Chapter Eleven

Owen was tapping a particularly stained mug with his pencil whilst humming some unfathomable tune when Cyril walked in.

"Still as musical as a stone trough, Owen. Don't give up the day job and if you keep drinking out of mugs like that you'll be booking a date with Dr Julie before me. It takes two minutes to wash it." He peered into it to see what appeared to be a fossilised tea bag lodged at the bottom.

"Washing the cup ruins the brew, Sir. Besides my guess is that there's some form of antibiotic in the residue." He smiled before picking up a report. "When Sadler went off the rails he derailed in a big way. Total train crash. Re-mortgaged his house, borrowed from friends as well as hitting the bottle. Eventually he embezzled cash from work, lost friends, lost his job and lost his home. According to the autopsy he also enjoyed cocaine. His family's now living with her parents, she works, kids at school. Her parents have supported them through the rough times."

"Do we have his records here, a photograph of a tattoo?"

Owen slid it across the table from the file. Julie was correct. Although damaged it was clearly Snoopy.

***

37, Moorside was a large, respectable, Victorian detached house. Owen rang the bell. The curtain in the bay window twitched and a short time later the security chain was slid onto the door before it opened just enough to allow the face of a gentleman in his late sixties to partially appear.

Owen showed his ID handing it to the man before introducing himself.

"Mr Baines? DS Owen and this is DCI Bennett. May we come in and have a word? It's about Drew Sadler."

Owen heard a deep, frustrated sigh as the door closed briefly and the chain was removed.

Swinging the door wide, Mr Baines looked at both men and they could see the anger in his eyes. He took them through to what he referred to as the parlour. Owen could see that he was on edge.

"I've bad news I'm afraid. You might want to sit down. Mr Sadler's body has been found. Could you tell us when you last saw him?"

Owen noticed immediately that the anger had returned as his seated body stiffened at the very mention of the name. There was a drawn-out pause.

"Must be twelve months since that bastard disappeared after taking everything from my daughter and the children, even took her engagement and wedding rings and the kids' laptop. Probably sold them to feed his gambling habit as well as his other sins."

Cyril looked up from his notes after underlining the word, 'SINS'.

"Good riddance, that's what I say. Not too Christian a philosophy, I know, but then we are talking about one of Satan's own."

The door opened and Mrs Baines entered. Cyril stood, allowing his foot to tap Owen's who immediately looked at Cyril taking the hint.

"He's dead is he? We can all rest. I don't suppose it was natural causes, probably not found in his own bed more likely in someone else's, caressing some cheap prostitute and a bottle of vodka?"

Both officers stood amazed at the immediate and forthright hostility shown by the petite pensioner.

"Could you please elaborate, Mrs Baines? His death doesn't seem to be much of a shock to you. We'd be grateful if you could fill in some gaps. We're interested in the period from when he started to go off track."

"Sit!" she barked, more an instruction than an invitation. "As far as I was concerned he was never on track. He did dreadful things to my daughter, and I doubt whether the children will recover fully from the trauma of seeing their father slowly dismantle their lives. It wasn't the first time in the relationship where he rocked the boat. I believe the worst for them was having strangers at the door threatening physical harm and damage to property."

"Mrs Baines, I'm confused. Could you go through the problems chronologically? I know this must be difficult and if you wish we could come back later to give you time in which to get your thoughts in order."

Cyril had hardly finished when she snapped back at him.

"Inspector, I want this out of the way with the minimum of fuss. Enough of Drew Sadler is certainly enough. They'd been married for a year when he had his first affair. Joan was pregnant with Gregory. He'd been promoted to manager of the supermarket and he had a dalliance with one of the checkout girls, but if you ask me he's always had a roving eye. I often felt as though he were undressing me when he looked at me and I'm no oil painting."

Cyril sensed Owen turn in his direction and then heard him cough as if stifling a laugh.

"You want to say something, Owen?" Cyril's voice showed his annoyance.

Owen shook his head, simply clearing his throat.

"Joan took him back but I think he carried on his lechery, maybe not with the same girl but probably there were others with eyes for their boss and hopes of promotion. I imagine there were prostitutes too."

"Did the threats you mentioned come from jealous boyfriends, husbands, pimps?"

Mr Baines, who had been silent interrupted, "No, they came from the people to whom he owed money. And believe me he owed a lot of money."

"Reg, go and put the kettle on I'm sure the Inspector would like a cup of tea."

Reg immediately stood and went into the kitchen. He glared at his wife, angered and frustrated by the way she had dismissed his input.

"Drew started to go to the local gym after work and on Wednesdays he'd call at the '*Running Horses*' on his way home afterwards, often until late. Joan grew concerned because she thought he was meeting a woman but he wasn't, he'd joined a poker group. I sent Reg in one time to have a look. He knew he was in because his car was on the car park. It seemed very innocent and once he'd told Joan they seemed better, they appeared more relaxed, happier. It was after this that things started to go wrong. The poker games went from one evening a week at the pub to two and then on the days he didn't work he'd disappear for a morning or afternoon. They stopped doing things as a family. Money suddenly seemed tight and Joan started to ask us for a few pounds for the children's school dinners or for school trips and then she noticed bills were not paid on time and that was unusual. Anyway, Joan discovered that the house was in the process of being re-mortgaged, that he had run up huge credit card debts and he'd even handed over the car logbook for cash to feed his gambling addiction. They began to argue and although she'll not admit it, I believe he was violent. It was then the phone calls started. They wanted Drew but when he obviously failed to reply strangers appeared at the house. On one occasion, he came home very badly bruised and knocked about. He told my daughter he'd had too much to drink and fallen but she knew. Someone threw a brick through the lounge window and if that was not bad enough a total stranger even called at Joan's work place demanding money. My daughter became very scared as you can imagine, Inspector, and extremely confused, so she came here and Drew stayed at the house. The final straw, as I'm sure you are aware, was his embezzlement of money from the supermarket, resulting in the termination of employment and a suspended sentence. It was then that he lost the house, it was auctioned by the building society and he vanished."

Reg arrived with the tea.

"So your daughter and the children live here with you?"

"She can still work and we can help with the children. Try to bring some stability back. Families need stability, Inspector, they need to be together, don't you agree?"

"So none of you has seen Drew since then?"

Reg coughed and spoke much to the annoyance of his wife. She folded her arms under her ample bosom and looked away.

"I saw him on The Stray, near Montpellier Hill, he was surrounded by his worldly goods; bin bags and an empty bottle. He didn't see me. I wanted to give him a piece of my mind but..."

"We'll need to speak with your daughter. It might be better if she came to the station. We shouldn't interview her here owing to the children, they've been through enough as it is. Thanks for your time. There's no need to identify the body as that's been done. We'll let you know when the coroner releases the body."

"We are neither interested in the body nor a funeral, Inspector."

"But your daughter might be to ensure an end to the matter. We'll discuss that with her. Please give her my card and ask her to ring me." Cyril spoke forcibly to ensure that she wobbled on her high horse.

Cyril was barely on the drive when Owen piped up. "Jesus, I'd drink and gamble if I had a mother-in-law like her! God knows what sort of life our Reg has, the guy hardly dares draw breath."

"Love and marriage, Owen, love and marriage. There's a free lesson in life about choice if you care to heed. Visit the *Running Horses* and see if you can get any names of people involved with the poker group. I know it was a while ago but see if anyone remembers Sadler and check if they're aware of any other poker nights run at different venues. Names, Owen, names! I'll call at the supermarket and see if any of the staff remember him. If they were there when he was, then they should."

Chapter Twelve

The long table in the incident room was carefully ordered. Displayed on one wall were a number of the images detailing the initial finding of the body, the autopsy and, at the top left, an unflattering police mug shot of Drew Sadler, taken when arrested for embezzlement.

Owen and Liz entered. Cyril frowned as Owen entered first leaving Liz in his wake before taking a seat and pulling a sheaf of identical papers towards him. Liz simply smiled at her boss, a smile that reflected everything Cyril was thinking.

Cyril looked at them both, Liz, petite and smart, was the total opposite of Owen who not only demonstrated a total lack of manners, but was also large and untidy. His plain tie, speckled and patterned with the remnants of some forgotten meal, looked almost designed that way. It was a good job dress sense didn't reflect his police work.

"Afternoon. No doubt Owen has regaled you with our visit to the Baines' household? To put it politely, I can concur that they were not exactly enamoured of their son-in-law."

"She wasn't enamoured by anything other than her daughter. If she could have got shot of her husband I'm sure she would," grumbled Owen.

"Cyril shook his head. Not necessarily true. Who'd make her tea?"

Owen laughed.

"However, they've filled in some gaps and created a more positive path for this investigation to pursue. What news at *The Running Horses*?"

Cyril picked up his pen to make notes.

"The landlord has been there for years and remembers Mr Sadler well and not too kindly either. The poker night was each Wednesday from 7:30 till 11:00 and from all accounts complied with the Gambling Act 2005. The group started small and gradually it proved popular with more and more people becoming involved. They were linked with pub tournaments. Sadler did well and was often the leading points scorer. Landlord said he was a big head and a pain in the arse. He was probably the keenest participant; he was always there at the start and remained until the last man left. The landlord had also heard that he'd got involved with some guys who ran a private poker game so you can guess that they weren't playing for points then."

"So if he was a winner in the pub how come he lost all the money?"

"My question exactly to the landlord. His experience suggests people play a different game when hard cash is involved, particularly when they can't afford to lose. They take greater risks, lose their confidence and basically and I quote, 'Flap and then flop'. Once they are in debt they bet bigger to try to recoup. He never saw this with Sadler because they were never in that situation in the pub, but he heard rumours. Losing a couple of hundred an evening was commonplace."

"Did he continue to play at the pub?"

Owen shook his head. "For about six months only and then nothing. He still heard some frightening tales, not just about Sadler but one or two others who thought they could win big. I've a couple of names and I'll follow them up discreetly. If they're heading down the same track, then we might be able to avert a similar crash. Should have been in Social work." Owen looked up and grinned.

"So no money changed hands in the pub?"

"Nope, just points. It's legal to have money games but it's heavily controlled, a limit of something like £5 per game per person. All controlled by the Gambling Commission. The advice is here."

Owen passed three stapled documents across the table.

"Thanks, Owen. So you'll check those names? Just add that to the board, there could be a lead. His last place of work didn't have many glowing words for the deceased either I'm saddened to say. From all accounts he was a lecherous sod, promoting those females who, shall we say, accommodated his interview techniques. One young lady told me he was always spouting on about how much he could win at poker, always flashing money. When he took her out one Sunday, they ate in style, champagne, good wine, the lot. She even told me that he had offered her cocaine after they had had sex in his car but she'd refused. Interestingly they all thought he was divorced, whether he said that or whether it was just assumed, we don't know."

"She took everything and then she obediently opened her legs even though she thought he was a total loser."

"Prostitution takes many forms, Owen. You know that."

"Let's not be quick to judge!" Liz shot back angry at the way the discussion was going.

"You're right, Liz," Cyril answered holding a hand up. "My apologies. So what do we have? He's a gambler, drinker, womaniser, manipulator, husband and parent. He's also arrogant, inept, insecure, immature, and to use Owen's term, a total loser who has been found dead under the strangest circumstances, a death that by all accounts was long drawn out and painful. Basically he was eaten. Liz, add those words to the board too. What are your thoughts?"

Liz wrote the words as Cyril read them again more slowly. She wrote 'No respect for women' at the end, underlining the words to demonstrate her annoyance at their biased, male opinions. She had said little since entering the room, her thoughts were constantly with the attacked child. When she had finished writing the last word she put down the pen.

"Funny, Sir, two people have been attacked by dogs, one lived, one died. At least in my opinion the correct one lived. Someone has used our man as an example, the attack was probably videoed and will be used to deter others from some activity whether that be failing to repay debt or some other intimidation. Could be mafia, could be triad, could be just a local drug gang wanting to elevate their standing in the community. We have enough possibilities with criminal gangs spreading from Leeds, York and Bradford, all wanting a bigger part of this lucrative, professional town."

"Owen?"

Owen stood and added a memory stick to a laptop and the screen image was projected onto an interactive board. He walked round to it.

"We even have our own Harrogate home grown baddies, don't forget. I did some investigating yesterday after it was suggested our man was more than likely killed by dogs. I know we hear of these attacks from time to time and usually the rare, fatal attacks hit all the papers but I assume that there is a good deal of hyperbole in common descriptions of dog attacks that really affects the reading or listening public."

Cyril looked round at Owen and raised an eyebrow. '*Owen's grasp of English was beginning to match his developing understanding of French,*' he thought and he jotted down the word 'Hyperbole', intending to mention it later.

"More adults die from being hit by a forklift truck or a runaway cow than they do from dog bites. So, the chances of being killed and eaten or partially eaten, by dogs today is exceptionally rare. Now for dogs to attack there need to be certain factors." Owen listed them all but emphasised four. "Dogs that are not neutered or spayed, the victim is compromised by ability, age or physical condition, mismanagement of dogs and finally, abuse or neglect of the animals, the report concluded that. Evidence supports that a number of these factors needs to be present for an attack to occur. So as far as I see it there is evidence to suggest that the attack was deliberate and the dogs were either prepared or trained for this purpose, as we haven't seen or heard of any other attacks, other than that on the child in a domestic situation. In that case we can assume that there were fewer factors. Those dogs have been destroyed so are of limited relevance to this process."

Owen took the memory stick from the laptop.

"Food for thought, Owen, food for thought. Good work. Copy of that and a reference on the board, please. The Pathologist is trying to determine the breed of dog by investigating the bite marks made on the body, but she has assured me that the strong bleach used on the remains might make that search of limited value. We have Joan Sadler in tomorrow morning at eight and I remind you that she wishes to be addressed as Mrs Baines. So, I should like you both and the team in here for a 07:30 briefing. Owen, send two of your lads to talk to your gambling names from the pub. I want reports on this desk for 07:00 tomorrow, if possible. Thanks and well done."

When he left the building, Cyril drew on his e-cigarette and the menthol vapour immediately made the muscles in the back of his neck relax. He stopped outside the gate and had a word with the security officer who politely asked if he were vaping in an attempt at giving up the real stuff.

"No intention whatsoever. Maybe when I retire."

He smiled and began his walk home. A dog barked in a garden to his left and his thoughts immediately went to Drew Sadler's final minutes. He felt a cold shiver slowly run down his back. He lifted his collar instinctively as if to form a barrier. He could think of nothing worse that being attacked by an animal, let alone becoming its next meal.

The traffic was now lighter than that morning and as he approached the junction where he had upset the motorist earlier in the day, he stopped to admire the *Zingaro* Restaurant. Workers were still busy. A small truck was parked in the car park and large sheets of plasterboard were being carefully manhandled through the doors. Another man whisked plaster in a large bath-like container with a drill and an oversized whisk. All carried the temporary evidence of their day's labour, coatings of dust. Light from inside the building had just started to leak onto the white, dusted cobbles that edged the car park.

Cyril lifted his coat sleeve and looked at his watch, it was 19:15. He shook his wrist and looked at the time again, he'd never got out of this habit. '*Late night*,' he thought. '*Must be on a deadline*'. He walked into the car park and stepped towards the door through which the workers were moving. He went inside, taking care to ensure that dust didn't get on his coat. The room was fully illuminated by temporary lighting, giving the space an austere ambience. The men seemed to ignore Cyril and continued speaking in a language, which certainly seemed to be Eastern European, which one Cyril was unsure. Other tradesmen were busy with plumbing, tiling and electrics. He began to walk across the room; nobody questioned him.

The interior was larger than he remembered it to be when it had been *The Beehive,* but then a number of walls had been removed giving a more modern, open space. Three men emerged from the area to the back. They stopped and looked at Cyril rather surprised that a stranger was so far inside the building. Angel and two other men were initially startled by the intrusion.

"Good evening, Cyril announced. "I was passing and as well as being nosey, I wondered when you hope to open?"

"No intrusion. Sorry for the mess, please mind your clothes. Thank you for your interest," smiled Angel concealing his anger that a total stranger had been allowed to just saunter in. "It will be my father's restaurant and we hope to open within the next fourteen days."

Angel moved towards Cyril ushering him back through the door he had entered.

"You're Italian?" asked Cyril in all innocence.

"No, my father is Chinese Romanian and I was born in Romania. We are Roma and that gives you a clue as to the restaurant's name. It will be beautiful and the food will be divine. My father will train all the chefs. You wait and see. Now you must excuse us we have much to do."

"Your workers are Romanian?" asked Cyril. "They are certainly making a lovely job of the place. I remember it as it was, a simple pub, *The Beehive.*"

Angel just smiled. "I'm sorry but we have much to do. Mind your clothes on the way out."

Cyril left contemplating the idea of an Italian menu designed by a Chinese Romanian chef. He shook his head. *In for a penny*, he thought.

Angel went back into the restaurant and smiled at his colleagues before looking directly at one and slapping his head.

"Nobody comes in, fucking nobody! You're supposed to be responsible for security." He slapped him again. "Jesus! Do I have to be here all the time? Do your job!"

***

The morning brought with it a stunning sunrise that grew in intensity as Cyril stepped out across The Stray. The dew jewelled the grass and he stopped to soak in the beauty. In front of his eyes the magic melted. The horizontal beams disappeared as the sun climbed behind distant trees and the glorious, vermillion sky became diluted. Cyril headed to work buoyed by the short, sublime interlude.

He was again surprised to see that the work continued at the restaurant. He wondered whether they had worked all night. '*They were certainly on a deadline*', he thought, '*and those guys must be making a fortune in overtime. No time to spend it but certainly earning it!*'

The briefing was exactly that, brief. Owen handed Cyril three reports on the other men who had started showing an over-zealous enthusiasm for gambling that had become unhealthy. He just noted their names, he would read the reports after meeting Joan Baines. He decided that Liz and he should interview Joan and that Owen should contact Forensics to see what other evidence might be gleaned from the body after Owen's research on dog behaviour. Their main focus was now on identifying the breed of dog or dogs involved in the incident.

Joan Baines was not at all what Cyril was expecting and it had to be said this misplaced idea of her threw him a little. Not only was she extremely attractive and petite but also she was open and gratified that they wished to hear from her. Cyril studied her and then thought of her mother, they were poles apart.

"This is the best picture I have of Drew, Inspector. It was taken just before things became difficult. I know my parents blame Drew for everything but then they would, wouldn't they? He was an attentive husband at first but when I became pregnant with my first, my hormones went berserk, my personality changed and I was cruel and unkind. That's when he had his affair. Anyway, we had another child so things did improve. The medication helped, I was prescribed anti-depressants, which proved effective but, like all things, there were swings and roundabouts. They had their side effects, not least on lowering my libido. So with pregnancy and then that, sadly he looked elsewhere."

Liz was amazed at Joan's resilience. She'd gone through all that, she'd faced the possibility of being homeless as money had been flushed down the gambling drain. The guy she had once loved and had spoken of with some affection had been tragically killed. She had her finger on the pulse, she realised why things had gone wrong and she apportioned blame fairly.

Joan explained that the gambling, the drink and the possible drug taking had begun to affect his moods; his desperation had increased when threats had been made towards the family. It appeared that all he had wanted was to face the consequences alone and it was Drew who had insisted that she go to her mother's.

Cyril mentioned the three gamblers' names and Joan knew of two. She had heard Drew mention them.

"Peter Anton was the one who always called for Drew or brought him home when he was either sober or drunk. He seemed very nice, looked after Drew. Once he brought me flowers when Drew had told him it was my birthday. If I'd not been married, Sergeant, I might have been tempted!" She smiled and raised her eyebrows as she looked at Liz.

Cyril mentioned the need for funeral arrangements and he was correct in his initial assumption, she did want to organise a funeral and expressed the hope that Liz and he could find time to attend.

"There will be few there as it is so we need to ensure we have some voices at his service. We know there will not be many tears."

Liz leaned across the table instinctively and touched Joan's arm. Cyril could see the respect Liz had for Joan even after such a short meeting.

"Sure," said Liz before turning to Cyril.

"Be honoured, Mrs Baines."

"As you may be aware, owing to the investigation, the Coroner has adjourned the inquest until criminal investigations have run their course so as yet we don't have a date for releasing your husband's body. This is, I'm sure you're aware, standard procedure. If our investigations fail to discover the facts surrounding your husband's death, then a second post mortem will be carried out and your husband's body will then be released. The Coroner's Office will be in touch with you giving you all the necessary information. I'm aware this is a very unsettling time for you and your family. One more thing, if I may. Why the name change?"

"Need you ask, Inspector, after all, you've met my mother! It simply makes life a little more bearable."

"One more question if I may, sorry. Did your husband have a tattoo?"

Cyril folded his papers as if anticipating the answer.

"The last time I looked, Inspector, he had my name tattooed on his bum, here," she pointed to her right cheek. "But as I say, he could have had 'War and Peace' tattooed since the last time I saw him naked."

Cyril sent the photograph of Drew Sadler for distribution in the hope that it might jog someone's memory. He poured a tea, made his way back to the Incident Room and settled down to read the reports on the three men that Owen had given him that morning. He wanted to pay particular attention to Peter Anton, although there was little in the report as time strictures had not allowed a full search. His gut spoke to him, and that piece of his anatomy seldom proved inaccurate. They might have within the flock a wolf in sheep's clothing. He sipped his tea and looked at the whiteboard. The last words written by Liz at the previous meeting had been erased and in their place she'd scribbled, 'A MAN!' Cyril frowned and then smiled. He looked down before underlining the surname of Peter Anton that was written on the sheet containing the three names.

Chapter Thirteen

As he lay on the bed, Rares' telephone vibrated in his pocket but it did not ring. Afternoon television bored him but there was nothing else to occupy him. He was neither welcome at the farm nor could he see Stella or Christina. He looked at the number displayed on the cracked screen and answered it immediately. His heart raced a little. As he listened he drew a head and face in the condensation that blurred the caravan's window He then added two horns reflecting his thoughts on the caller. He had said barely three words when the phone went dead. He erased the image of Satan and left.

The small green van was waiting as instructed and Rares climbed into the passenger seat.

"Fuck, I've been so bored. How are my dogs?"

"They haven't missed you but we've missed your not being with them. We need them, three of them, in two days' time. The appointment is in the city and Angel wants them ready and more importantly he wants them winners."

The driver turned to look at Rares and his expression said it all. There was little emotion in his eyes, they were just deep, cold pools of expectancy and Rares knew this meeting had to go well.

The dogs were caged in a small barn to the south of the main farmhouse. When Rares entered they neither showed excitement at his presence nor did they acknowledge their minder's return. They simply collided with the mesh hard, the way they did when anyone entered the dark barn, each of the dogs displaying a line of hair along their backs standing upright, a warning of their intentions. Rares smiled knowing his dogs had reacted well. The aggression was still there. He put the back of his hand against the mesh and his scent triggered an immediate excitement. The scarred heads of all the dogs showed their fighting pedigree; two had lost ears and one sported deeper scars, two ugly chunks of healed flesh on its rump. It was as if they sensed that they would soon be working. Rares moved to the far wall and collected the carcass of a rabbit that was hanging by its trussed hind legs from a rusting nail. He banged it against the mesh causing some displaced fur to fly through it and the dogs eagerly snapped at the gossamer offerings before all five dogs stood passively when instructed. They knew what was to happen next. Saliva dripped from their chops, as on cue, Rares moved his hand to unclip the hook and eye attached to the small gate. He began to slide the gate, set high in the cage, slowly to one side before tossing in the carcase. Its flight never had a chance to touch the ground, within seconds there were only pieces. More loose fur was launched into the warm, turbulent mass of air above the dogs. There was no barking, only the aggressive snarl as one dog dominated the others. Although King was not the biggest dog, it was certainly the most aggressive and feared by the group. That night, Rares would inject the animals with steroids, a routine he regularly undertook to ensure optimum muscle bulk and aggression.

From today the dogs would be on a limited diet and they would be separated to ensure that each received just the correct amount of food. They had to be hungry and they had to be able to fight. He looked across at the mechanised treadmill he had set up in the corner. The dogs were at their peak.

Suddenly Rares felt as though he were being watched. He looked around but there was nobody in sight. He had not heard the door but he sensed that there was another person present.

A voice from above in the hayloft made him jump. "The dogs look good, my friend even though you've neglected them."

Rares looked up "Jesus Christ, you scared me."

"Your guardian Angel, my friend, not Jesus Christ. He would not live here amongst our kind."

He was surprised to see Angel laughing at his own joke, his feet dangling over the edge; beside him was a young woman.

"I knew you'd be missing Stella so I've brought you a gift. She's yours for the afternoon as a token to show you that you're still loved. She's OK, I've tried, she's new, speaks no English. Picked from the streets and the silly bitch believed, until last week, that she's here to work only in the new restaurant. If she's good and works hard then she will but if not, she'll earn money in other ways. So just in case, my friend, we have to get her used to different men and their different needs. She's a favourite of Cezar's." He turned to her grabbing her cheek. "Can't keep your hands off him can you girl?"

Angel jumped down from the hayloft and the dogs hit the mesh, eager to get at the men outside. Angel smiled at the dogs' reaction.

"Did I ever tell you about my first dog?" Angel dusted the straw from his clothes and fastened the fly buttons on his jeans.

Rares shook his head wondering anxiously what was to come.

"It was a gift and his name was Lupei. Like me, he was young, but that's where the similarity ended; he was so brave and I was so scared. He was given to me to protect me, a friend when I thought I had no one. I believed then that he'd only protect me but, I was so wrong. I learned then, at a young age, that not everything is as it seems and that lesson has helped me in my life. You see, Rares, Lupei did just what his master said and if he told the dog to protect Wadim then that's what he would do, nothing would pass him, not even the master. If he were to approach, he would be attacked. But if Lupei were told to watch me then I could not move. My dog would attack me and bite if I moved just as much as this." Angel moved his little finger close to Rares' eyes and made it twitch a fraction. "The same with these dogs. You've trained them well. We have a big night coming up and we need to make money. These beautiful dogs will do that for us. Enjoy the girl but don't damage her."

Angel grabbed Rares' cheek and squeezed. It was then that Rares realised that there was no real affection in the words nor in his gesture, only threat.

"Oh and when you've finished with her upstairs, take her to the bunk house and then come to the farm, I need a little chat with you about Stella."

Rares knew that the smile did not bode well and any inclination for sex drained quickly from him. Suddenly he felt a deep unease.

***

Liz noticed Cyril sitting at his desk, his head back and his hands behind his head. His feet were stretched out to the side and were crossed at the ankle. She noticed the shine to his shoes, even between the sole and the heel seemed polished. Her eyes were then drawn to the immaculate creases to his trousers and she smiled.

"Sir, the Emergency Care Order has been granted and Christina will remain at the hospital. The mother is allowed to see her, human rights and all that crap. I'm liaising with the child's solicitor and guardian to ensure that she will only go back to Stella when she is clear of booze and drugs. That shouldn't be difficult and it will arm us with the necessary Service Providers who will then take an active role in the little one's welfare."

Cyril swivelled round to his desk and picked up a file.

"I want you and Owen to interview Peter Anton, a bit of a character but one of the guys who was also identified as having a fondness for poker. I got the impression that Sadler's wife had a bit of a soft spot for the guy. She assured us that nothing was going on, but who knows? Maybe you also felt as though there was more going on than she was admitting?" Cyril paused and looked for Liz's reaction but registered nothing. "Run a check, see if you can come up with something and pay him a visit."

***

Rares, as he had thought, found no pleasure with the girl who seemed to reciprocate his lack of passion with a motionless, tearful performance. He looked at her before offering the rag from his pocket to dry her eyes. He spoke gently in his native tongue and she smiled. He drew her towards his shoulder and for the first time he felt her relax.

"I'm so scared," she whispered. "This is not what was promised. It's not true about Cezar. He lies."

Her accent was unusual, refined, she seemed educated but at the same time so naïve.

"How long have you been here?"

"In England? I came with the first rush in January. We were all so excited. A new life, more money and better jobs but I didn't find things easy. I ended up sleeping rough. After a while, fellow Romanians helped me. I suddenly had work, it was only washing up but it was work and I had a safe place to stay but that quickly changed. It was as if I had become a possession because I had accepted help, they said I had a debt to repay. When I tried to leave I was threatened. It was then that they raped me. I was brought here, wherever here is!"

She started to cry again and her hands began to shake. She wiped her eyes with the rag.

"I've not been able to call my home unless someone is listening. I'm told what to say and how to say it but mainly they make me text messages to my family. I write what they tell me. I can't go out on my own. I'm in prison. They allow me to collect benefits but I'm with two others who are watching and listening. I never see the money, it's taken. Now I'm here, trapped and scared. You are the third man to fuck me today."

Rares looked at her and felt ashamed. "I'm sorry. Like you I'm trapped. I do what others demand. I've seen what they will do if you refuse. See those there?" Rares pointed to the dogs. "They are the punishment for not listening, for trying to leave, for not doing as you're told. What's your name?"

The girl looked at the dogs and then focused her brown, wet eyes on Rares. "My name's Sanda but here I'm Sandra. When I finished university I thought that all my hard work would be rewarded. How wrong I was! Nothing back home is as bad as this."

Rares felt her arms tighten around him and for the first time in what seemed forever, he became alive and human. Her tenderness lit a small flame of anger inside him, warmth that he had not felt for some time. If he could, he would try to protect her he promised himself. If he couldn't protect Christina then he would do his utmost to protect this girl. He leaned down and kissed her tenderly on the forehead.

"You will never have to be afraid of me again, Sanda. I am sorry for hurting you."

The tears returned as she relaxed and for the first time he saw her smile. It was as if the tears and the smile had re-humanised Rares if only for a brief moment.

***

Liz and Owen stared at the computer that furnished them with Anton's details. Each looked at one another and then back at the screen.

"Curiouser and curiouser!" cried Liz. "Sorry, not good English but from my favourite book. They seem to be crawling from the cracks in the pavement. He's lived in the UK for the last five years. First year at the University of Leeds, Master's degree in Accounting and Mathematics, now working within Jones and Croucher International Accountants, Leeds but lives near Follifoot."

"Date of birth, 1984. Born Petev Anton in Bucharest. Father killed in the '89 Revolution. No details. Mother remarried six months later and the family moved to Constanţa. She was off the mark quickly. Are you thinking what I am?"

Liz looked around and smiled. "Revolutions are a great way of getting rid of unwanted baggage."

"Wars and revolutions are great for settling old scores and getting even." Owen scrolled down but he found no other details.

"He works, pays his tax but gambles. He looks clean. I'd like a check on his Romanian past. So often we're finding that many of the legitimate migrants have skeletons in cupboards so I'll get that sanctioned. Let's pay our man a call."

***

Liz and Owen walked up the drive before stopping at the parked, white Skoda estate. Its engine ticked and clicked as it cooled. Owen put his hand on the bonnet. It was still hot.

"Just home if my senses don't deceive me."

"I can see why 'Flash' likes working with you…always on the ball," Liz said cynically. "A real detective will give me the exact time it was parked."

Owen stuck his finger in his mouth to wet it and held it in the air. He pulled a strange face. "18:21 and," he paused before looking at his finger, "…thirty-three seconds."

Liz simply smiled and hit him on the arm. The door to the house opened before they even had time to reach it.

"It's not for sale." Peter's face remained slightly threatening.

"Peter Anton?" Owen said as he moved to the door as if countering the threat with his bulk. He neither liked Peter's facial expression nor his manner. It was as if he were being taken for a fool. He took out his ID and put it close to Peter's face, which flushed and changed to a look of surprise.

"I'm sorry. Just noticed you around my car. We've had a few stolen recently and thought I'd show my face."

"We need a brief chat. May we come in? This is DS Graydon."

The room was tidy, if a little minimalist. A modern abstract painting hung on the back wall and a flat-screen television was positioned on the chimneybreast. Neither seemed straight. Strewn papers littered a small coffee table and from what Owen saw they looked like accounts. A half drunk mug of coffee rested on a coaster.

"Homework, Mr Anton?" Owen said as he sat.

Peter collected the sheets. "You know, work goes on even after the company clock has stopped. There's always someone prepared to take my place if I don't meet my targets."

"What can you tell us about Drew Sadler?"

Owen watched Peter's expression closely.

"He's a friend. We go out occasionally. We both like to play poker at the pub, or shall I say we did. Haven't seen him for a while. He suddenly stopped phoning. I've been busy at work…

year-end and all that so I've been tied in here as you can see. Is there a problem?"

Liz interrupted. "How well did you know his wife?"

Owen noted a reddening in his complexion again before he answered.

"I knew her through Drew, that's all. When I collected or took Drew home we'd speak and when Drew was having some financial trouble I'd help."

"Sorry? Help? How?"

"She asked me to look at her accounts. Suddenly there was no money when previously there'd always been enough. Drew had started drinking a little too much on occasion and let's say he was growing rather profligate. He suddenly found that he had an expensive hobby. I'd lend her a couple of quid now and again when I could see things were really tight."

Owen noted the word *profligate,* he would investigate its meaning later.

"How much is a couple of quid?"

"The most was a hundred. She said she'd pay it back but…"

"Have you ever been intimate with Joan Sadler?" Liz stared directly at Peter as she asked the question.

"What sort of bloody question's that? What are you insinuating?"

"It's a question you ask about a woman who was so recently widowed. Did we not mention, Mr Anton, that Drew Sadler is dead?"

Peter's expression changed, first to shock and then to anger. "What the bloody hell is going on here. Sadler's dead? When? How?"

"I'd like you to come with us for further questioning. You'll be cautioned but you're not under arrest and you're free to go whenever you wish. We're only asking for your honesty and co-operation. We're simply trying to put together a picture of Drew Sadler's final days. Mr Anton, there might have been foul play involved in his death and can I say now that you're not, at this moment in time, a suspect, just an acquaintance who might be able to shed a little more light on the man. There are two other men known to us who played poker with Drew who will be interviewed and like you, they are simply friends of the deceased."

Liz watched him frown. He chewed the fingernail on his index finger as his looked around the room. He was clearly anxious.

"How long will it take? Could we not do it here?"

"We could." Liz produced a Dictaphone and put it on the table. "We need to record this."

Peter nodded his agreement and sat down. He took a deep breath.

***

Rares left the girl by the bunkhouse and walked up the cobbled track that led to the farmhouse. He stopped in the stone porch and stared at the oak-studded door. A brass knocker, depicting a sitting Alsatian dog, faced him. He knocked once and after what seemed an age the door opened and the youth with the marks to his forehead looked at him.

"Angel wants to see me."

Angel was sitting in the kitchen, his feet on a carved Chinese chest. Ancient, wooden beams spanned the width of the room like nicotine ribs attached to a large, sternum-like central beam twisting its way along the room's length. Hanging from this were small, tasselled Chinese lanterns. The fire grate was empty other than for the grey ash residue of a previous fire.

"Well? Marks out of ten for the girl?" Angel looked up but showed no expression.

"Thanks… I enjoyed her." His voice was flat and expressionless in an attempt to camouflage his true emotions. Rares pictured her face, particularly her dark eyes awash with tears. This somehow gave him strength. "Can I keep her at the trailer until I can meet with Stella again? I'll take her with me to the Kebab House and watch her."

Angel didn't take his eyes from Rares. "If the dogs win, then maybe I'll give it serious thought. I'm glad you mentioned Stella.

Sit!" Angel pointed to the chair opposite and Rares sat. "You'll meet Stella in Leeds tomorrow night, briefly, that is. She'll be at Jo's café. She needs things. Christina won't be released from hospital for at least another ten days, they've taken out a care order and that's put Stella in pieces. She's not functioning and a number of her regular punters haven't been pleased with her performance. If they're not pleased then we're not pleased. We're a family after all. Am I right?" The question was rhetorical giving no time for Rares to answer. "You'll give her a package and then leave. She trusts you more than anyone else."

Rares knew that the package meant drugs or money for drugs and he chewed his lip, his anxiety unknowingly displayed across his face.

"Will the police not be monitoring her? What about watching me?"

Angel shook his head. "They've more to do than worry about you both, after all, the child is their main concern and she's safe in the short term. They've seen you've formed a routine and that your papers and tax are in order. Why should they waste resources on a gypsy nobody? You'll be in Leeds with the dogs. Twenty minutes to see her and then back to work. We'll ensure Stella's safe. Now check the dogs and get back to work." Angel checked his watch. "You'll be late."

***

The incident room was quiet as Owen and Cyril stared at the white board.

"Never underestimate the feeling in your gut, Owen. It makes for a good copper. I knew there was something not straight with Anton."

Owen could feel his rumble but knew it to be neither intuitive nor inspirational. It was hunger. He'd missed breakfast and right now his intestinal juices were sending him a timely reminder.

"Was that you, Owen?" Cyril had heard the protestations too.

Owen nodded. "Missed breakfast, Sir."

Cyril went across to his jacket and removed a nut health bar from the pocket. "This was for my healthy lunch but from the discussion going on in there," Cyril pointed to Owen's gut, "your need right now is greater than mine will be at twelve. So, Peter Anton might have had a reason to see Sadler hit the buffers, to use your train metaphor?"

"He says that he helped Joan try to sort out her finances as well as loaning money and his idea of a few quid was up to a hundred. Some accountant!" Owen took another large bite from the bar leaving only the wrapper.

Cyril lifted his eyebrows before inhaling the menthol vapour from his electronic cigarette. "And you said the debt was still outstanding?"

Owen nodded. "According to Anton she never paid it back and he hasn't been in touch since."

"There's more to this than meets the eye. I want him in for questioning. Say it's to eliminate him from the enquiries but I want him in. I want DNA as well. I also want the reports from the Romanian Police through sharpish. The other two only look to be associated with the pub game. One no longer plays and although he was acquainted with Sadler, he had little to do with him. I'll leave them on the board but I think we've reached the end of the track with those two." Cyril smiled as he watched the significance of his sentence float over Owen's head.

Chapter Fourteen

It was late afternoon when Rares arrived. He was checked at the gate and then dropped off at the barn. He took a stun baton from the safe and attached it to his belt. It was designed specifically as a defence against dog attack. He could never be too careful, the dogs, once excited and frenzied, could be unpredictable. Quickly, he muzzled the three dogs before putting them into their transport cages. Two men lifted them into the back of separate cars. It wouldn't be good to be stopped with the dogs in one vehicle, particularly on the return run. Dogs that have fought were not too pretty and their discovery would take some explaining. He moved back to the safe in the corner and removed a wooden box before placing it on the table. He lifted the lid and removed the heavy, metal object. His hand expertly checked the captive bolt gun before returning it to the box. This would be needed if any of the dogs suffered too much. He went to the van putting the box in the cage with the dog.

The destination would only be sent by text at the last minute but the drivers knew the general destination near to Leeds City Centre, each having been given Sat Nav co-ordinates to follow. They would leave fifteen minutes apart and with luck arrive at the chosen venue at different times. Rares would be in the lead car. He would need to be there to check the dogs. He also had to see Stella. It was estimated that the journey would take less than an hour so there was no need to leave until after five. The traffic would be heavy at that time, but usually it was leaving and not entering the city.

Rares sat and looked around the barn. His thoughts moved to Sanda as his eyes scanned the hayloft. He left the barn and walked quickly to the bunkhouse but she wasn't there. His stomach sank with disappointment and the thoughts of what the poor girl was being forced to do. He returned and waited in the lead car. The dog smell permeated the car's interior but somehow that was comforting. He seemed these days to spend his whole life waiting! Angel and the three drivers chatted by the farmhouse before they ambled to the cars. The driver smiled as he climbed in and Rares despaired, it was Cezar, a man who was quick to react and not to be trifled with. He had grasped the Anglo Saxon elements of the English language well and he was renowned for his use of a blade. Rares feared him; he had witnessed his anger and the type of justice he dispensed.

"To the fucking smoke, yes!" He tapped the steering wheel as if it were a drum. "I hate fucking green fields and sheep. Crowds, crowds with deep pockets, that's what we want."

Rares noticed when he smiled that he was without two front teeth and that his nose had been battered at some time in the past. He noticed too that part of his left ear had been removed. He looked a real hard case.

Once on the outskirts of Leeds the driver monitored his speed with extra care. They travelled down Scott Hall Road and onto Eastgate before rounding the City Centre Loop. Rares felt his heart flutter as the Police Station loomed into view on the roundabout.

"Rozzers, the bastards!" yelled Cezar with honest hatred as he banged the steering wheel again. "Fuck 'em all! It'd be good to put one or two with the dogs. The pigs would really squeal!"

Crossing the river, the driver pointed to the Leeds Armouries. "Great place to visit if you like old guns and that shit. They've a beaut in there, it's called a Welrod, used as a silent assassin's weapon. Real Second World War, SAS stuff. Saw one in Bosnia when I was there helping, so to speak. Would love one. There are a few people I'd like to kill fucking silently."

Rares ignored him, strangely tired of the language and watching the road he wondered if the boasts were only bravado, if his bark was actually worse than his bite. He decided that he wouldn't like to find out. Within five minutes they were parked on Sweet Street and the Sat Nav. announced that they had reached their destination.

"This is as far as we fucking go until we get the text."

Sitting enclosed in the van, Rares was enveloped in the canine smell and the sound of Cezar's rhythmic breathing. His eyes were closed, his peaked cap over his face. He was trying to sleep. The surroundings were desolate, the revenge of the industrial revolution's aftermath. Streets once lined by mills and factories were now littered with the flotsam and jetsam, so often dumped within the empty demolition sites that scar modern cities. He saw neither birds nor animals, just the ragged remnants of man. The cobbled street, a fossilised, pachyderm skin, was all that was left apart from twisted iron railings and the occasional broken lintel, partially concealed by gangly buddleia and grass.

He thought about the promises he had made to himself, his ambitions on leaving his home country, his parents and siblings. These thoughts, these aspirations had slowly eroded like markings in sand, washed by the tide of time. He felt disappointed, angry with himself for his entanglement with others but his inner guilt told him it was surely his doing. He wasn't forced to be there, not at first. It was easier and more convenient initially. He welcomed the company, the hospitality and the promises of a better life, the life he had originally envisaged. It was the new life; it was the independence for which he yearned. Maybe he'd find an English wife, have kids and possibly be able to afford a house and a car of their own. He had Stella, she was sort of English, and she had Christina. He knew that Christina didn't belong to him, it was just that he wanted to believe it, he wanted the child, a beacon of hope, he wanted someone, someone innocent, someone to truly love. He knew too that he was ensnared and that the further he became embroiled, the more strongly the trap would grip. He'd seen what happened to people from 'the family' who had tried to escape. He had seen what the dogs did in error in the tunnel. One day that could be him, or Stella or Sanda and, although it wasn't cold, he shivered.

He could go to the police and confess everything. They already suspected that he had done wrong, staying at Stella's, but they'd listen surely. He had names and might even be rewarded in some way, then again maybe not. If he told of the tramp's annihilation by dogs he had worked with there could only be one conclusion… prison and prison with Angel and Cezar filled him with absolute terror.

Cezar's phone signalled the arrival of a text and his stream of thoughts stopped instantly. The orange-streaked sky and the extended shadows brought visual warmth to the dismal street. Butterflies tumbled in Rares' stomach as Cezar turned and greeted him with a sneering grin.

"Game fucking on!"

He tapped the address into the Sat Nav.

"Eight minutes from here. We have to arrive at seven. We'll wait ten minutes and then go."

Rares looked back and checked the dog, it too had responded to the sudden excitement in the car. It stared back, its bead-like eyes eager for action. The other two cars would be planning their arrival time as instructed.

Cezar started the engine and began to drive following the spoken instructions and within the given time, a row of arches beneath the railway came into view. The road passed under a steel bridge before disappearing to the left. The first four arches, each with a small walled yard to the front topped by a mesh and barbed wire fence, were bricked up apart from steel garage-style doors within the brick façade. Rares recognised a youth from the farm on a bike riding up and down the street. He then noticed the hand-painted sign, 'Archway Autos'. This was it. The youth pushed open the gate and moved towards Cezar's window.

"Drop off in the yard and then park away. Here…" He handed Cezar a scrap of paper on which was written an address.

Cezar drove into the yard. Rares climbed out and the two lifted up the cage. The garage doors opened and Angel appeared. He beckoned them with his hand. In the shadows of the viaduct, it was

www.tesco.com

VAT NO: 220430231

Thank you for shopping with us.

TESCO

Every little helps

Should you change your mind about your
purchase, please return the product with your
proof of purchase, within 30 days, and we'll
happily offer a refund or replacement.

Conditions apply to some products.
Please see instore for details or
visit www.tesco.com/returns.

Tesco Stores Ltd
Tesco House
Shire Park, Kestrel Way
Welwyn Garden City
Hertfordshire
AL7 1GA
www.tesco.com

VAT NO: 220430231

Thank you for shopping with us.

TESCO

Every little helps

Should you change your mind about your
purchase, please return the product with your
proof of purchase, within 30 days, and we'll
happily offer a refund or replacement.

Conditions apply to some products.
Please see instore for details or
visit www.tesco.com/returns.

Tesco Stores Ltd
Tesco House
Shire Park, Kestrel Way
Welwyn Garden City
Hertfordshire

98146

ESSO 98764

SHEFFIELD FULWOOD EXPRESS
any questions please visit
www.tesco.com/store-locator

PUMP #3 DIESEL

70.84 litre @ 153.9 P/L   £ 109.02C

TOTAL   £ 109.02
MASTERCARD DEBIT   SALE £ 109.02
  AID   :A0000000041010
  NUMBER   :************7164   (ICC)
  PAN SEQ NO :01
  AUTH CODE :301932
  MERCHANT   :5
  START DATE :07/21
  Cardholder PIN Verified
  Please retain for your records

VAT RECEIPT SUMMARY
GOODS

Rate	NET	VAT
C 20.0% VAT	£ 90.85	£ 18.17

ESSO VAT NO: 239088635

CLUBCARD STATEMENT
CLUBCARD NUMBER   ***************0293
POINTS THIS VISIT   36
POINTS BALANCE   525

19/08/23 14:11   3135 080 3   3130

740   322   246·4

now quite dark. The dog was placed inside. The space was larger than it appeared from the outside. It had an arched, brick roof that reminded Rares of 'The Darkie', the Harrogate tunnel where he had witnessed the tramp's death. A single bulb glowed near the entrance.

Angel grabbed Rares' sleeve. "Leave the dog and go see Stella. Give her this and remind her she owes me. You've thirty minutes. You know the café? Opposite the cash and carry, yes?"

Rares nodded, took the small, padded envelope and left. He watched Cezar reverse the car out of the yard and disappear round the corner under the bridge. A train, comprising two carriages trundled slowly overhead. It was getting dark.

***

The café was squeezed between two modern industrial units well inside the estate of warehouse buildings and small factories that cluttered a portion of the North East area of Leeds. The flats silhouetted the surroundings like dormant concrete sentinels adding to the grim atmosphere. Rares knew the café well; it was a regular meeting place when he came to the Chinese Cash and Carry just across the road. Its paifang, the Chinese-style gate, formed the entrance, all curled ends and red tiles, a beauty spot on an ugly face. On either side were positioned the two dogs of Foo that guarded the entrance. He remembered being fascinated by them as he was with all dogs.

Stella was waiting, a mug of coffee steamed in front of her on the red Formica table. The bell rang as Rares opened the door. The other two occupants sitting at tables took no notice and it was only Stella who reacted. She turned to look at the person who had entered. There was no smile, no small wave, no sense of connection. She simply turned back to look at the coffee. Rares walked over and sat. The cloying smell of fried food hit him and if he had felt hungry before he entered, his appetite soon deserted him.

"How are you?" He slipped his hand on top of hers but she moved away. "I've been worried. I heard that Christina has to remain in hospital for a little longer. It'll be all right in the end, it has to be. You're a good mother, Stella."

"Your dogs, you bastard, that's why all this has happened. Everything would've been fine if you'd just listened to me. They should have been away when them pups arrived."

She looked at him and he was amazed how plain she looked. Her hair seemed unkempt and dirty matching her nails that were chewed.

"For Christina's sake you need to clean up your act. You can't do drugs and booze and expect to keep her."

He hadn't finished when she stood knocking the table. The coffee spilled and ran in a thin stream off the edge of the table and onto his crotch. He jumped too.

"Shit!" He brushed off the liquid with the back of his hand whilst tossing the package onto the table. "For you."

The two people looked from across the room and then got on with reading their papers. You didn't stare too long in places like this. He checked the time on his phone; he had twelve minutes to get back.

"Got to go. Take care." There was little sympathy in his tone.

Stella simply took the package and sat back down.

By the time Rares returned to the railway arches, several people were seated. Laughter occasionally echoed in the large, vaulted space but generally the conversations were muted. All seemed to know each other, there were no strangers. Caged dogs dotted the periphery of the room, each cage being covered by a thick blanket. Rares dressed quickly in a white, paper boiler suit, it was always messy in the pit. Angel pointed to him and beckoned him to bring King. They washed the dog and the opposition followed suit using the same tub of warm water before drying the animals. Once King was back in the covered cage, Cezar helped him to carry it through more doors into another room. Inside was the makeshift, square wooden, scratch-built 'pit' spanning approximately fifteen by fifteen feet. The floor was carpeted in red. Improvised lighting hung above the centre of the pit, similar to that in a boxing ring; its intensity shadowed in secrecy the outer edge of the wooden walls and the twenty or so punters who eagerly entered to take up position on the outside. The walls were higher than for normal fights, as these dogs were bigger. For Pit Bulls the walls didn't need to be high. A referee stood in the centre. Thick gloves covered his hands and he held a breaking stick to help separate the dogs should he feel the need. The two scratch lines were marked across the corners showing the separate start positions for the dogs. Two, doors were closed behind the lines. The caged dogs were brought up to the doors. The blankets were removed. The excitement grew amongst the spectators and the dogs instinctively tried to attack. The betting was frenzied. The dogs were held behind the scratch lines ready to be released, ready to be scratched.

Inside the pit were the dogs, the handlers and the referee. At a signal, the dogs' muzzles were removed in readiness for the start. Another call presaged the release. There was no foreplay. Both dogs sprinted at each other biting and snarling, splashing blood being the initial result. It was neither pretty nor dignified. King's strength was the more impressive and quickly the dog turned its opponent over and went straight for the neck, tearing and ripping. Blood speckled those who cheered close to the pit wall. The handlers separated the dogs to give the weaker dog some time before rereleasing it. Nobody wanted the fight to be over too quickly. Within seconds King had turned the other dog a second time. The underdog had given in, bitten badly around the eye and neck. It screamed and instinctively stopped fighting hoping that its opponent would also stop. It was its last hope. King continued to rip even though it had stopped kicking and struggling. Its legs twitched spasmodically. King continued to attack as if angry that the fight was over too swiftly. Rares grabbed the dog by the soft flesh at the side of its neck and pulled it away. Initially, the dog continued to tug at the lifeless leg of its opponent. Rares pulled a hessian sack from his pocket and covered King's eyes before pulling again. With the other handler inserting the break stick, he managed to get the dog to release. They moved King back behind the scratch line. Rares threw some meat into the cage, pushed the dog in and the door was closed. Rares bent and whispered to the dog through the cage. His expert eyes were carefully assessing for any damage to his animal. It had a large rip across its left jowl, cuts to the snout and front legs but he would glue and staple these injuries later; an antibiotic injection would also be administered. Blood continued to dribble onto the cage floor from the larger wounds. The noise from the spectators was intense as money changed hands in eager anticipation of the next fight. Rares felt Angel pat his back.

"Well done, we missed you."

Rares said nothing just smiled and went back to his dog.

Cezar left the building, chatting briefly to the watchers before going to collect the car. He waved at the youths who continued to watch for any unwanted intruders along the street. Within fifteen minutes the dog was loaded and then he left, leaving Rares to manage the other two fights. Rares would return with the last dog.

Chapter Fifteen

The fast response paramedic vehicle screamed up the A59 out of Harrogate. Vehicles moving to the side of the road allowed it swift passage; it was all lights and sirens, its destination being the layby at Kettlesing Head. A call had come in to say that a woman was having breathing difficulties and needed urgent assistance. Other information was sketchy. A large, articulated wagon was positioned on the left of the sweeping, half-moon shaped layby that was once part of the original road. As requested, its hazard lights flashed repeatedly. As the estate car came to a halt, its blue, flashing strobe lights overpowered the yellowy-orange flash and illuminated the dark lane, the bushes and the trees that formed a hedge between the main road and the resting place.

"She's in here! I don't know if she's breathing! Shit come on!" shouted the panicked driver. "Christ! Christ! Help her!"

As the paramedic sprinted from the car, a second siren was heard, like a whispered echo, way down towards the lights of Harrogate. The ambulance was lumbering up the hill towards them. It would take another two minutes to arrive, but it would prove to be two minutes too late.

Stella was on her back on the cab's bunk, her skirt above her waist and her T-shirt rolled down exposing her breasts. Within seconds the paramedic was administering CPR.

"She was fine, she suddenly stopped breathing, her eyes rolled back. It was fucking scary and she didn't move."

The paramedic heard but didn't respond, he was far too busy breathing for the woman and he didn't rest until his colleagues arrived. Within seconds, a traffic police vehicle pulled in and parked, obstructing the entrance to the layby. Cars travelling by were already slowing to allow their occupants to rubber-neck. The wagon driver lit another cigarette and paced the tarmac next to the wagon as the medic continued his treatment.

"Are you the guy who made the call? Are you OK?" the police officer shouted as he walked over to the wagon.

The driver took a deep breath and shook his head.

"What's your name, Driver?"

"James, James Nolan but I'm called Jim."

"Come and sit in the car, you'll be suffering from shock. She's in safe hands. They'll stabilise her before she goes anywhere. There's nothing now for you to do. We got the call that a woman was in difficulties. What happened?"

"The taxi dropped her off as usual and she was fine but suddenly she started to choke like. She threw-up and started to have a fit like. Ya know what I mean? I couldnae stop her and then she just went still. I couldnae hear her breathing. Ya know what I mean?" His strong Scottish accent seemed more pronounced the more anxious he became.

"A friend of yours was she, Jim?" The officer watched the driver's expression. "Known her long?"

The driver just nodded and put his head down. "Stella often meets me when I'm in the area. Know what I mean? I ring and if she's available, she gets a cab up here."

"Was it paid sex?"

The driver nodded.

"How often is often?" The traffic policeman waited for 'you know what I mean?' to appear at some stage within the sentence.

"About every six weeks. I'm divorced see and I know she's clean. To be honest, I really like her too; she chats and seems interested. Know what I mean? Remembers stuff, about me and I like that. My wife never did, she was only interested in herself."

James looked at the cab. "Surely they should be getting her to hospital. She must be stable now."

"It takes time, trust me. Now is the critical time. It's no good moving her until she's stable."

The paramedics began to move from the cab, the rings and loops on their clothing reflecting in the vehicles' headlights like some macabre dance. They were slowly extricating Stella before gently placing her on the gurney that was jacked up at the door to the cab. Jim could see she had oxygen and various tubes disappearing beneath the blanket that covered her. Within minutes the ambulance was pulling away, blue lights illuminating the side of the articulated wagon. He heard no siren.

The police officer called for another vehicle to transport the driver to the station and also for a Scene of Crime Team.

"I cannae leave it," James said pointing to the wagon. "Company rules." His eyes were worried.

"Does the company allow you to entertain ladies in the cab, Jim? Or have you bent the rules? Give me the keys, I'll lock it and believe me, it will be secure this evening."

Forty minutes later, the Crime Scene Team was entering the cab. The lay-by was closed off and temporary lights were erected illuminating the wagon. It would be a swift review. If drugs or signs of a crime were detected, the cab would be seized. Jim was already in the Police Headquarters; he was alone apart from a cup of tea and his thoughts.

***

Cyril was awake early. He dressed and decided to skip breakfast. He tapped his jacket pocket to ensure his wallet and glasses were there. '*Spectacles, testicles, watch and wallet,*' he whispered to himself. It was something he had always heard his father say on leaving the house and he had carried on the tradition, the religious connotation never really crossed his mind. He looked at his watch shaking it and checking again. It was 06:50.

Owen arrived early too and entered the briefing room to find Cyril straightening the photographs and papers on the white board. Everything always had to be just so.

"Got a call to say Stella Gornall was rushed into A and E last night but died earlier this morning. She was 'tricking' in a wagon up on the Kettlesing Head Lay-by. 999 call at 23:17. Driver is a James Nolan from Innerleithen, that's…"

Owen didn't finish the sentence; he had noticed the familiar expression on Cyril's face, the look he fired when someone was stating the obvious.

"I know where it is, Owen. It's on the A72 between Peebles and Galashiels. Now get on with it!"

"Sorry! They believe drug overdose. Know more after post mortem." He looked at the sheet of paper. "They found a padded envelope containing a significant quantity of tablets and two packs of cocaine in her bag. Being tested. There was £325 in used notes too. Forensics also found a number of condoms, litter and a small plastic bag identical to the other two on the grass separating the road from the parking area."

Owen handed the sheet to Cyril.

"What do we know from the driver?" He looked quizzically at Owen. "Nolan?"

Owen shrugged his shoulders. "Just what's on the sheet, Sir. They met whenever he was in the area. He told the officer that they'd met up about six or seven times. He'll be questioned this morning."

"I'd like Liz involved in that interview. She'll need all the info about Stella to liaise with Social Services about Christina. What about the Romanian boyfriend, have you brought him in for questioning?"

Owen looked at Cyril. "She wasn't with him. In fact he hasn't been at the house nor the hospital. I'll send an officer up to chat with him, break the news."

Cyril just raised one brow. "Either the drugs came from the driver, or from another source. I want him in today."

Owen realised the conversation was over.

"And Owen, let me know when he's here."

***

The police car was parked outside the caravan and two officers walked round checking the doors and windows. Rares and Cezar watched from a safe distance.

"You expecting the fucking Fuzz?" Cezar said as he spat out of the window before wiping his mouth on his sleeve.

Rares shook his head. He thought immediately about Christina and his stomach sank making him feel nauseous. Cezar didn't wait. He turned the car away and headed back to the farm. He knew for certain that Angel would not be too pleased. The farm gates swung open and Cezar parked the van in the yard.

Angel simply stared at the two men.

"What's he back here for?"

"Coppers looking around his place. They didn't see us so thought it best to come here. We checked that we weren't followed." Cezar spat again. "Fucking hate the Coppers, me."

"Have they paid you a visit out of the blue before?"

Rares shook his head. "I've not been to the hospital nor to Stella's as you instructed. I just go to the kebab shop and my trailer, work and sleep, you know that."

"Cezar, take one of the new guys to the kebab shop to work in place of Rares who, I'm sad to say is going to disappear for a while."

Rares suddenly felt vulnerable on hearing the word 'disappear'. Beads of perspiration showed on his forehead and his gut tightened. He knew what happened to people who endangered the family. Even the slightest risk would not be tolerated.

"I've done nothing wrong, Angel. You saw how the dogs worked last night. It's probably Christina, something's happened to her."

Angel nodded. "And if it has, what then? They were your dogs. It'll mean a prison sentence for somebody and the police snooping could just be the start. You understand that the family comes first. At the moment, my friend, let's not jump to any conclusions, let's wait and see. Don't ring or contact Stella. I'll check on the hospital."

He moved and rested a hand on Rares' shoulder; it felt more threatening than reassuring.

Angel had hardly finished speaking when his phone rang. Angel's face changed, he looked puzzled then frowned before his eyes locked on Rares. "When? Keep me informed."

Rares now felt certain he was an obstacle. "Is it Christina?"

Angel pulled his lips together and shook his head. "It's that bitch of yours, it's Stella. She's dead. Last night."

Chapter Sixteen

Jim sat motionless, a dark two-day stubble coated his chin and from the look of his tired eyes he had had little or no sleep.

"So you say the taxi dropped Stella off at 21:45 or thereabouts? She seemed fine when she arrived apart from being a little cold? You gave her some coffee and brandy but later she seemed worse. You told the officer attending…" He looked down at his notes and read. "Here it is and I quote, '*she seemed to be not herself*'. You chatted for a while and you left the cab for a pee. When you returned she was just adjusting her clothes. Was she removing them?"

"She never took 'em off, if ya know what I mean. Only her knickers anyway, the rest rolled up or down. That's the way it had to be and it was OK with me. She wasn't herself, that's right. She had a sore throat she said and we stopped sex because she said she was painful down there. To be honest, it wasn't really the sex, for me it was more the company."

"Yes, you said that." The officer looked at Liz hoping to draw a cynical smile but she didn't respond. "You weren't worried that she might be infected?"

"It did cross my mind, Aye."

"Did you pay her even though the sex was poor?"

"Aye, she trusted me. Like I said, I always paid for her and her taxi back."

"Did you use a condom?"

James for some reason blushed. "Aye."

"What did you do with it?"

"It went oot o' window. Sorry!"

The officer couldn't help but smile. A woman had died in his cab and here he was, apologising for littering.

"Did she take anything, tablets, cocaine?"

James shook his head. "I didnae see her take anything but when I came back from having a piss there was white around her nostrils. I know she's a user, why else take money from guys like me?"

Liz looked hard at James and she thought she saw real compassion in his expression.

"Did she ever mention that she had a child, James?" Liz asked, softening the questions and trying to make him relax.

"Aye, Christina I think her wee lassie was called. She showed me a photograph. She was real pretty."

"You really liked Stella didn't you?"

"To be honest, she said that we might soon be able to live together, if you know what I mean? Move up to Scotland and live. I've a hoose. I wouldnae want much. Maybe she would stop taking stuff if she had a fresh start, like. We talked about it a few weeks back. She said she was having difficulties with her fella, he's a foreigner she told me, Romanian I think but that's all I know about him, bit of a bully from all accounts. To be honest with ye, Stella didnae look well. Her skin wasnae as good as usual and she looked all washed out but I put it down to her partner being a shit, like."

Liz looked at the other interviewing officer and their eyes confirmed naivety and foolishness, but also some respect for the man sitting in front of them. It was clear that he had strong feelings for the deceased. She checked the paperwork and noted too that he had no previous police record which supported her intuitive belief that he was with the wrong woman at the wrong time.

"We'll need DNA samples and fingerprints but you know that, James. If you want, we'll test to see if you've picked up anything else. It shouldn't be long until we know the cause of death. We've contacted your company and they're collecting the trailer. We're keeping the unit for further forensic work. You'll be released on bail pending further enquiries but after today you'll be free to go. One last question, did you always contact the same taxi firm to collect her?"

James shook his head. "Nae, Stella organised a drop off and a pick up. She wad call when she was ready." He hung his head and began to cry.

"Who dropped her off?"

"Couldnae tell ya. As I've said, Stella booked that taxi, I just gave her the money when she was in the cab."

Liz made a note to check Stella's phone for numbers.

***

Cyril read the toxicology report on Stella. It showed that the drugs she was carrying were key factors in her death:

'*The cocaine was heavily contaminated with Levamisole, a veterinary drug used for de-worming farm animals. Most samples of street cocaine contain some. In this case it resulted in neutropenia and agranulocytosis which had gone undetected, leading to a sudden fever and septicaemia. She died from a resulting cardio infarction. The skin showed clear evidence of purpura, again a result of the ingestion of Levamisole. Clear evidence of alcohol dependency.*'

Cyril picked up the phone and dialled Julie Pritchett's mobile. It rang four times.

"Sorry, wasn't as quick as a flash in answering that!" She emphasised the word 'Flash'. "What can I do for you Cyril?"

Cyril detected the laughter in her voice. "Very droll, Doctor. I find myself with another body, that of a young woman. Let's hope they don't come in threes. Toxicology shows heart attack from an overdose of contaminated cocaine. My question is regarding Levamisole. Is it only used to de-worm farm animals or is it used in domestic animals too?"

"Good question, ask me one about sport!"

Cyril laughed out loud. "For that you must come out for dinner, but only if you answer the first question without asking the audience."

"Yep, it was but not now. It was used to treat heartworm in dogs. Did I pass?"

"Flying colours."

"What's the name of the young woman?"

Cyril replied and Julie promised to take a look at the notes and get back to him.

"One last thing. The Snoopy tattoo on the guy's backside, could there be another tattoo underneath?"

"Could be I suppose. Would you like me to take another look?"

"Always the star. Thanks, Julie."

Cyril walked over to the white board and wrote down Levamisole before drawing an arrow to Rares Negrescu's name. "Dogs yet again!" he said out loud.

"Sorry, Sir. Didn't catch that."

Cyril briefly explained. Owen informed Cyril that there was no sign of Negrescu and that after interviewing the owner of the kebab house, it appeared he had rung in sick the previous day. According to his boss, this was unusual, as he never took time off.

"Let's not make two and two into five, let's just be cautious. You've someone checking the caravan on a regular basis?"

Owen nodded.

**

The following morning Cyril and Owen called at the lab. The full forensics results on the cab and the detritus found around the cab had not been completed and would take the best part of four days if they were to prioritise. However, they had an interesting find on the envelope. They had discovered dog hairs stuck to the self-adhesive.

"The hairs were not cut but were telogenic, meaning they were shed. Shed hairs can play a key role in forensic investigation as we have now developed better systems of analysis." Cyril looked at the young lady who seemed barely old enough to sit her GCSEs but then she probably thought that he was Methuselah.

"We have identified the hairs as coming from a Rhodesian Ridgeback."

Cyril felt his skin tingle, the same breed that had attacked Christina.

"Could they have come from the same dogs that were in Stella's house?"

"We checked samples taken from the dogs before they were destroyed but they are not the same. Same breed, Chief Inspector, but the dogs these hairs came from…" She held up the transparent packet… "have been fed a diet of anabolic steroids. Toxicology shows Stanozolol. It would strengthen the animal. It's really a performance-enhancing drug."

"Have you seen that before?"

"Common in the dog fighting world."

Cyril rubbed his chin and turned to look at Owen. "We need Negrescu and we need him quickly."

Owen nodded. "You were right, Sir." He pointed to Cyril's stomach.

Cyril just tapped his gut and smiled. "Something you don't learn, Owen. You're born with it!"

***

The information from the Romanian Police files regarding Peter Anton proved interesting as Owen flicked through the printed email and sighed. He walked to Cyril's office and tapped on the door.

"You'll not believe this but our friend Peter or shall we say Petev Anton has an interesting past. Spent time in prison for GBH. He attacked his stepfather with a hammer. The sentence was reduced on the grounds that he was protecting his mother from his violence. Also had one or two minor run-ins, mainly connected with youth gang culture but then he seems to have settled down after his prison sentence, university and then over here. I still cannot understand how we just accept people into the system with criminal records."

"They've been abusing the system for years. Murderers, prostitutes, pimps and vagabonds have all managed to find their way here. What's sad, Owen, is that nobody realises that they are here until the proverbial hits the fan. It has to be said that a lot of good citizens arrive too, but they never make the front page of the newspapers. I don't believe the Government has any idea of the numbers working legally or illegally what with name changes and document falsification. There's money to be made controlling these people who are, in many cases, desperate, particularly if they have a limited command of our language. Don't forget that our benefit system is the most generous in Europe, if not the world. Most come as self-employed which gives them the same access to tax credits and housing benefits as any other, its benefit tourism. Now, shall we say, less wealthy EU members can enter the country legally and take up employment without authorisation. Take, for example, those poor builders working down at what was '*The Beehive*', they never stop. If they don't put the time in, there's always someone willing to replace them. Just look at the number of migrants sleeping rough and multiply that for each and every town and city! Beggars belief! And don't forget, they haven't stopped coming. Look at the streams pouring through Europe. Stories circulate at home of allowances and benefits that make their own hand outs seem paltry. Too easy with Job Seekers' Allowance, money for housing…"

Owen could see Cyril's face grow redder the higher his blood pressure rose, which seemed directly proportional to the height he achieved on his soapbox.

"How did he support himself when doing his post graduate studies?"

"He found employment in a variety of food joints whilst studying at Leeds. No criminal record there. We know the rest, of course. I'd like to know how he funded his Masters' Degree if he'd been inside before his move to the U.K. Find out all the establishments in which he worked, if his employment and tax records are accurate for the period he's been here. That shouldn't be too difficult. Also find out with whom he associated whilst at University, his accommodation etc. When you have that we'll chat with him. What about Negrescu?"

"We've watched his caravan but nothing, no coming nor going. He's still not at work, the owner of the Kebab shop tells us that it's most unusual. He still has some of his wages and according to him, money is the one thing that Negrescu wouldn't leave if he were planning to quit. I'd like to get clearance for a forensic search of the caravan sooner rather than later."

Cyril seemed calmer. "I'll sort it."

***

Owen was surprised that the list of Peter Anton's temporary employment was not as long as expected for his year at the University. It appeared that he tended to work at a local Chinese takeaway or in a Chinese Cash and Carry near Burley, not far from his student accommodation. It was easy to track those who had shared his accommodation at the time and Owen had six names. The local Bobbies could interview them wherever they might now be; standard police procedures. He would visit the cash and carry himself and he was also keen to know more about Anton's present employers and possibly their clients. He knew that gleaning that sort of confidential information would need greater leverage than he could bring at this present time.

***

Cyril and Owen watched as the dog handler moved around the caravan. There was no movement from inside.

"Take the dog away!" Cyril instructed.

Cyril pointed to the Forensics' team. An excited Spaniel was brought forward as the Alsatian was taken away. They moved towards the caravan accompanied by two officers. The black ram made small work of the door lock sending splinters of plywood on a path of least resistance that finished at the officers' feet. One officer checked the caravan quickly and once he was sure that it was empty inside, he moved aside to allow the Forensics' team entry led by the drug sniffer-dog.

It never ceased to amaze Cyril how quickly spectators appeared once the plastic tape cordon was in place; already four or five people observed from the periphery. The four police vehicles positioned along the path to the caravan was the draw. Owen went over to the group and made enquiries but they had not seen the owner for several days.

"Keeps himself to himself. See him come and go, never see him in the shops. Bit of a miserable bastard if you ask me, foreigner too."

"Does he have a dog?" Owen asked the lady who had a scruffy-looking Poodle on a lead.

"I've never seen nor heard a dog here and I live over there." She pointed to the end-terraced house in the small row. "So you'd think if he had a dog I'd know. I often let Cindy-Loo out for a pee at night and if I thought there were other dogs about I wouldn't. You can never be too careful. What's he done, any road?"

"Gone missing!"

"Probably milked enough out of our system like 'em all and then buggered off home."

Cezar just watched from the back of the group. He rolled a cigarette in his fingers, deliberately showing little interest in the proceedings; he lit it before turning away. Owen saw him turn to leave and, for some reason, he felt he should speak to him; it was something about his appearance or maybe his height. Owen lifted up the tape and went after him.

"Excuse me." Owen put his hand on the man's shoulder and he felt him stiffen and turn aggressively, blowing smoke into Owen's face. He turned his eyes to look at the hand on his shoulder and then looked down at Owen, something not many did. Owen removed his hand and showed his ID.

"Why are you here?"

"Just being fucking nosey, saw a few people so thought I'd come and see what the fuss was, see. You one of them detective type coppers? Has somebody died?"

Owen smiled. "Have you seen the man who lives in the caravan in the last couple of days?"

The man nodded. "Not in the last few days but seen him before, now an' again like, tends to say nowt. Best way really if truth be known but I've not seen him here for a few days. As I say just stopped today for a piss."

Owen looked at the man's facial damage, his part removed ear and his missing teeth. Although the man had a local accent, he knew that he was of eastern European descent. It was difficult to determine his age, but he guessed mid to late forties.

"You live local?"

"Stopped for a piss as I said and then saw the cop cars. Wondered if I might help but then seeing everything seemed right, thought I'd bugger off or am I breaking the law?"

"Where's your car?"

Cezar pointed up the track.

"Owen!" Cyril called and gestured that he should come and look.

"Thanks for your time." Cezar turned to go. "Is this the man you've seen here?" Owen asked, holding out a photograph for the man to take. Cezar didn't touch it, just nodded, turned and carried on up the lane.

Owen watched him toss his cigarette butt into the hedge. His vehicle was behind the police vans but Owen managed to glimpse the colour. He had wanted him to touch the photograph but he did not. He had a strange feeling about this character but he did not know why and having a fingerprint might have been an advantage. However, he would soon have the cigarette butt and that should be one in the bank. Forensics would retrieve it shortly. Any DNA recovered would be checked against the UK National DNA Database. With luck his hunch would prove positive, if not it would be stored alongside the description added to and referenced to HOLMES.

Cyril held up a plastic bag containing two bottles and some new syringes. The bottles were without labels but the contents would be analysed. Forensics had also retrieved dog hairs from items of clothing. There was nothing else of interest; in fact, the only personal items were three photographs. One depicted a wedding couple and judging by the age of the photograph and the clothes worn, it could be assumed that it was Negrescu's parents. The second was of Stella and the baby. Strangely, the third was of a dog.

***

The sky was grey and a slight drizzle greeted Cyril as he left the Police Headquarters. He put up a small umbrella, waved at the security officer on the gate and wandered down Otley Road. His thoughts tumbled uneasily as he catalogued aspects of his day's work, reliving conversations and observations, weighing the information and running it through his mind. The repetitive noise of the tyres on the wet road made him switch off from his musings. He stopped to look at the progress being made at the restaurant. Things were busy. He was just about to carry on when he heard a shout.

"I see you most days either morning or evening heading past and I wanted to give you this." Angel handed Cyril an envelope. "It's an invitation to the opening night. You seemed interested when you called in and I hope you will do us the honour of attending. Please also bring a guest. There will, I feel sure, be a few problems, tooth problems you say?"

"Teething problems," Cyril corrected politely. "They are only to be expected. That is very kind. I should like that. Thank you. And your name is?" Cyril held out his hand.

"Teething problems, yes but let's hope not too many." Angel smiled and took Cyril's hand with a firm grip. "My name is Angel, and you?"

"Cyril, Cyril Bennett."

"Tell me Mr Bennett, do you work up there?"

Angel pointed up the road. He had assumed that Cyril worked in some capacity at the Police Headquarters.

"Yes, I'm a police officer for my sins. That's what makes me nosey." Cyril smiled.

The answer did not surprise Angel, if anything it excited him. Now his enemy was going to be closer still. "Please come. There is a number on the card so you can let us know if you'll be attending. We must know how many to cater for and stop any… teething problems." Angel smiled.

"Thank you, it's very considerate of you. You mentioned that your father was training the chefs. Is all going well?"

"My father arrives tomorrow. I'll introduce you at the opening."

Cyril turned, gave a brief wave before continuing his walk to Robert Street. He smiled inwardly thinking that the new apprenticeships would be pretty whirlwind. Maybe you didn't need many skills for Chinese, Romanian or Italian recipes.

The house seemed cold when he arrived home. He switched on some music, opened a bottle of Genesis beer followed by the envelope. Cyril checked the calendar and picked up the phone. The beer was wonderful; he had discovered it at a beer festival held at Harrogate Town Football Club; it had become a firm favourite. He settled down and admired the painting in front of him.

"Julie, it's Cyril. How are you?" Her reply suggested that it had obviously been a bad day.

"Cyril, some news on your dead girl. Stella had been consuming contaminated cocaine for some time looking at her liver results. She was in a very bad way. Usual STDs too, Cyril, so your driver's idea that she was clean was a myth. Suffered from an enlarged heart bringing about heart failure. This is quite common amongst alcoholics as I'm sure you're aware." She paused awaiting Cyril's protestations, which came on cue. "It's also a symptom of serious drug misuse. She probably suffered from arrhythmia too. For her age Cyril, she wasn't pretty."

"The thought of all that's just given me an appetite for my evening meal. Smashing! I've just put my beer down and to think I only rang to ask you out for dinner at the opening evening of the new restaurant I mentioned a while back."

"Sounds lovely, when?"

"Week tomorrow. I'll get a taxi and collect you at..." Cyril looked at the invitation. "Is seven alright?"

"Looking forward to that and no corpse talk, promise? By the way, nearly forgot, there was evidence of a tattoo beneath Snoopy. Script lettering spelling 'Jean' or 'Joan'. I'll add it to the report."

Chapter Seventeen

There were eight officers in the briefing room when Cyril stepped through the door, his electronic cigarette in one hand and a bone china cup and saucer in the other. It looked out of place amongst the water bottles and mugs that had been left on the table by his colleagues.

"One day you will all see the light and realise tea and china are totally compatible." He smiled, inhaled the vapour and relaxed into his chair.

Owen started the briefing. "We've not got all the details back but a couple of the students who were in the same halls of residence as Peter Anton tell the tale that he was a keen gambler even then. Thought he had it worked out mathematically, and even though he was working in his spare time, he had debts."

"Doesn't every student?" Cyril responded whilst sipping his tea.

"One guy, a Carl Jones, told the officer that he was threatened by some guys regarding a fairly large amount of money that he owed. When questioned he seemed to remember that they were of Asian origin. This might be the reason he worked predominantly in the Chinese trades. Was he paying back debts?"

"You went to the Cash and Carry?" Liz asked.

"Yes, he worked for them most weekends, usually in the accounts. It was all above board too. They were pleased with his work, so much so that he was employed by them immediately after finishing University until he got a permanent job at the accountants, Jones and Croucher. It was for about six months."

"Where did he live after Uni?"

"According to his employers, he was sharing a flat with two students. Just a second…" Owen flicked through his notes.

"Yes, here it is. The flat was in Chadwick Street. Actually, when I checked, they're very posh apartments that look onto the canal. It's near the Armouries. Not cheap by all accounts but some middle-eastern students often rent there so it's not unusual. I thought it strange but if he were being paid well it shouldn't have been a problem, particularly sharing."

One of the officers who'd been chewing a pencil for most of the briefing made a solitary contribution. "Who were the flatmates?"

"We don't know at this stage but that's being looked into. It shouldn't be difficult to find out providing everything was above board. If he were crashing on someone's couch, we've no chance. I've requested the names of all tenants for that period and we'll see if anything shows. I'll pass that task to you to chase, Stuart." Owen looked at the officer chewing the pencil and smiled.

"Remind me to keep my big mouth shut," he grumbled with a smile. The others around the table giggled.

"Anything to add Liz?" Cyril asked as he finished the last drop of his tea.

"When we interviewed the driver of the truck, he informed us that Stella organised the taxi to and from the meeting. It's logical. I've checked her phone records and there is no taxi company number on the phone. I've one number that appeared on the night in question but it's now discontinued! Obviously a buy and throw card."

"Your feelings about the truck driver? Honest? Straight?" Owen asked.

"He seemed genuinely concerned about Stella. Even the attending officer and the paramedics suggest that if he wasn't, he should win an Oscar."

"We know where he is and we have bail set."

***

The maroon Mercedes 4X4 slipped down the slope and turned onto the platform leaving the Eurotunnel train; it was five minutes early. Hai Yau looked across at his wife and smiled. As usual, she held a small dog that was curled on her lap. It was

101

going to be a long drive. They had planned to arrive at the farm by four in the afternoon but that would depend on the motorway traffic and the number of stops needed to let the dog and his wife piss. France was so much easier with its tolls and predictable traffic. They had spent the night at the hotel Suite Novotel at Sangatte , ten minutes from the Eurotunnel check in. Hai Yau could not help but feel excited at the opening of, in his eyes at least, his most expensive and contemporary restaurant. The ones in Romania ran themselves, he had a good team and those in Yorkshire were beginning to be profitable but all were really only fast food establishments. This was a step up, in both direction and clientele. His workforce too added to his coffers.

To Hai Yau it was his reputation as a local businessman that mattered most, a businessman who was seen to have charitable links that were growing; sponsoring local children's teams, donating to the local hospice, all found the news; he was ring-fencing. Slowly but surely he was creating the façade that he needed in order to hide the less savoury elements of his life. It had been easy in Romania, money talked and blind eyes were turned; in England money still talked but in a far more subtle way.

One thing both he and his wife had missed was their son, Angel. He smiled to himself at the thought of the little boy who had been brought to his house, a little boy with a brave face but with tears in his eyes. He then thought of the beautiful young man he had become. Hai Yau felt the warmth of pride swell within him.

The Yorkshire roads were quiet once they had left the busy motorways. Within half an hour they would be home. Hai Yau rang the farm from the car phone and Angel answered.

"Welcome, welcome home. We're ready for you. I'm sure you'll want a shower and a good meal and then we'll catch up. Drive safely."

The farm gates opened with a press of the remote and the Mercedes pulled into the yard. Standing silhouetted in the stone porch was Angel. He brought his hands in front of his chest as if in prayer and bowed deeply before running to open the passenger door.

***

Rares paced the solitary room. His anxiety grew by the hour. He had heard that the police had searched his trailer and he knew Angel's father was due; a man he most feared. To Hai Yau, he knew he was dispensable. He was also worried for Sanda. He had glimpsed her briefly as she was driven away but she had failed to see him. She looked tired. Suddenly his imagination became his enemy, he thought of her being forced to have sex with a number of men and he shuddered, he could neither sleep nor rest. He concentrated on an image of the trailer's interior, mentally searching the surfaces and cupboards for anything that might connect him to the dogs. He remembered the syringes and bottles and began to sweat even more. If Angel were to know, it would be the end.

***

The gates to the farm opened and father and son drove towards Harrogate. Although Hai Yau was tired after his journey and meal he desperately wanted to inspect his new restaurant. Work was still ongoing. Only small, decorative jobs that seemed to take the most time and consume the most cost, remained outstanding. As they turned off the road, the restaurant car park was almost clear apart from one lockable skip. Two men swept around the outside and stopped to inspect the car as it entered.

"We've nearly finished but the lighting and the floor were so expensive."

Hai Yau looked at his son. "Remember, my child, that cheap things are not good and good things are not cheap. This has to be the best, the best staff, the best food and as you have seen, built with the best materials. You've done well. I need to see my kitchen for it is in there that the magic will happen."

Angel stood amazed that after all these years his father had lost none of his enthusiasm for cooking. He led the way, walking in before standing beside the stainless steel work surfaces. He turned to his father and noticed the man was weeping. He paused and lowered his head.

"We shall bless it tomorrow and the training will begin. My staff is ready, yes?"

Angel nodded. "They are in the accommodation at the rear, they're especially well looked after and keen to begin."

"I'll see them in ten minutes. Have them here."

Angel moved swiftly as his father ran his hands over the surfaces and opened the fridges and drawers. He had worked hard for this and his mind reflected on his first ever restaurant and he smiled to himself.

"You've done well, Hai Yau," he whispered to himself as he wiped away another tear.

Angel led nine people into the restaurant and he introduced his father. They stood in a line before him. He bowed and smiled.

"I'm pleased to say that you've been chosen to work with me in this wonderful kitchen. The word sounded more like chicken."

He stopped speaking English after seeing the quizzical expressions on some faces and spoke in Romanian.

"We'll make wonderful meals together. The work will be hard and the hours long. Everything must be perfect, including you, and you and you..." He stopped at Sanda. "You cook before, girl?"

"Yes, at home, but not the food of the Italian people."

"You will or you'll not cook at all."

He went down the line and looked into each pair of eyes that held a sense of fear of the unknown. Each began to wonder why they had allowed themselves to be brought here but then, memories of sleeping rough, of only occasional work, of not knowing where the next meal would come from, suddenly seemed a far cry from their present, privileged position. What could be worse than the gut wrenching fear felt in those cold, dark, early hours on the streets of Bradford or Leeds?

"If not, my friends, you'll no longer be here, you'll find yourselves working elsewhere and not one of the chosen few as you are now and certainly not with the benefits. For here, as you have seen, you've good beds, you'll eat well and there'll be money to send home, more than you're used to. Most importantly, you'll slowly become trusted, you'll learn skills." He paused. "But with that trust comes a responsibility to my family and to me and should that trust be broken, no matter how insignificantly, the consequences will be very serious indeed. You'll be on call at any time. You'll be clean and tidy and this kitchen will be the cleanest in Harrogate. We start tomorrow with cleaning at 6am. Does anyone not want to be here? For now is the only time you get to change your mind. We have five days to be ready."

Heads turned to look down the line but nothing was said.

He waved his hand to suggest they could return to their rooms.

Angel didn't want to spoil this momentous occasion in which his father was revelling, so decided to keep Rares out of the conversation until the following day when they both could digest the implications of the police visit.

Chapter Eighteen

The police car dropped Jim by the bus station. His bail had been set and there was nothing else he could help with. Besides, he had a new job to find once he returned home. He could have taken the train but that would have been costly. There were four buses daily travelling between Harrogate and Edinburgh and this would do just fine. He stopped and bought a meal deal and two cans of lager before sitting on the bench to wait. He looked at the bay number. It was 13, just his luck or not as the case might be. It was quiet. The coach was due to leave at 11:35 stopping at Newcastle at 14:00 with an hour wait and then on to Edinburgh. It seemed a long journey but he was in no particular rush, after all he was missing the one thing that he had come for. After fifteen minutes, a large gentleman came and sat next to him. A peaked cap almost covered his face. Jim had failed to notice his approach or see him take his photograph on a mobile phone before he sat down. Jim turned and could not help but focus on the disfigured ear.

"Angel sent me to say thank you for keeping your gob shut. He asked me to give you this and said that if he sees you in this neck of the woods again…" He paused and looked at the ground. "You'll not be leaving vertically." He turned and grinned, his toothless smile said it all. "If you know what I fucking mean. Seeing the fucking taxi didn't return for Stella there was no way to get it to you."

He handed Jim a plastic carrier bag. Jim looked at it and back at the messenger.

"I hope it's all here. Tell Angel that's more than fine by me. He has no worries on that score unless this is the same quality of shit that did for the lassie in ma truck 'cos if it is, its na only me you'll be getting a visit from. I take it he received the payment intact otherwise I wadnae be holding this or having this chat with ya now?"

Cezar only nodded and stood. "Not as thick as you look."

"And big guy, should we ever have to meet again, I'll be happy to remove the rest of your fucking teeth. I might claim the other ear too, if ya know what I fucking mean."

His Scottish accent seemed to emphasise the threat as he pronounced the word 'I'." He locked eyes and refused to turn away. Cezar could only fume inside. It was rare that anybody, particularly someone much smaller than he, would dare to retaliate either physically or verbally. He spat on the floor in front of Jim.

"I have people who would pay to see that, pay good money." Cezar smiled and turned. He knew all too well that he could neither cause a problem nor go against Angel's wishes. At that moment the National Express coach pulled in front of them with a squealing hiss of breaks. The engine was switched off.

"An tell that Angel chappy that I'll clip his fucking wings too if I ever meet him!" Jim's voice carried across the station and a number of people turned to see who was shouting but Cezar was gone. He heard nothing. Jim stuffed his meal deal into the carrier and waited for passengers to get off before helping an elderly lady climb the steps. He followed her before settling into a seat half way down the coach. Three other passengers got on, all men. One stayed near the front and two came towards the rear occupying the seat directly behind Jim. The seats in front and next to him remained empty. The coach would leave on time. Jim pulled the ring on one of the cans.

***

Peter Anton had pulled into a layby on the A61 near Ripley and checked his watch. Jeremy Vine droned on about cracks in the walls of buildings. Peter flicked the stereo to CD mode and Jeremy was replaced by the calmer tones of The Eagles; they were half way through singing 'Hotel California'. He settled back to wait, his eyes scanning the rear-view mirror as his fingers drummed the steering wheel lightly. It was then that he saw the familiar car indicating to turn in. It pulled up behind. Peter smiled and raised his hand to wave.

As the passenger door swung open, Peter grinned at Joan. She climbed in, leaned over and kissed him passionately, her tongue penetrating his lips.

"God I've missed you," she pronounced.

***

Cyril read the latest toxicology results detailing the residue in the containers found in the caravan and it seemed to make perfect sense. Everything had pointed to abuse from the word go. Yes, there had been errors, the police and social services should have responded to concerns more quickly, the evidence was now, in hindsight, clear to see. The child unattended, the mother, addicted to god only knew what, the dogs, the kennel-type room. The one mystery that continued to plague Cyril was Rares Negrescu. Where did he fit in? He neither was the child's father nor legally attached in any way and yet he obviously cared. Liz didn't believe he faked the concern, it was palpable, she felt it and Cyril trusted Liz's instincts.

He continued to study the results. The containers had held the anabolic steroid Stanozolol. The dog hairs found on clothes in the trailer also tested for the drug as well as being a match, *from a Ridgeback*, to those found under the adhesive of the envelope held by Stella and yet they were not a match to the samples taken from the dogs that were removed from her home.

After a further briefing it was decided to put out a wanted notice for Negrescu. He was responsible for the injuries to Christina and he could have been responsible for her death if luck had not been on the little girl's side. If he did have fighting dogs and he was on the move there were obvious dangers to the public. There was also the idea that he might have been dealing the tainted drugs. Surely the evidence was there and from what he knew about Negrescu and his connection with dogs, anything was possible. Within twelve hours it would be on the local news and social media. It should not take long to locate him. Owen had organised the incident room to be fully manned. Full press coverage to mobilise public assistance always resulted in an influx of calls; regrettably the majority would be of little help.

***

Hai Yau returned from the restaurant after a full morning with the staff. He felt confident that they would work well together. He had left them cleaning and he would return that afternoon to prepare for their first cooking experience. He went to shower and eat before meeting Angel.

***

The prefabricated cabin was still as cold and intimidating as the first time he had sat in this very chair. However, on this occasion, there were two chairs facing him and nobody holding on to his shoulders. The sun broke through the thin cracks around the ill-fitting doorframe, penetrating the gloom with sharp, white needles of light. Rares watched the dust float in circles as if trapped like aircraft in powerful searchlights before disappearing as the light quickly faded. His thoughts turned to his trailer and the syringe and bottles he had stupidly left. His mind again traced the contents of the trailer. Had he left anything else? He shook his head. He didn't think so. The door opened and Angel and his father walked in. He stood instinctively and for some reason bowed his head towards Hai Yau. The gesture was returned. They spoke in Romanian.

"So, I've heard that the police have paid you a visit. It was, we feel, an unnecessary visit that has come about through your carelessness, Mr Rares. Is that so?"

Rares looked at his feet and then back at the two men. "I've always tried to do as you've asked. The dogs are good are they not? They are proving to be winners. I work hard and keep out of trouble."

"What could the police be interested in? Why would they possibly want to search your trailer? What is it that they want? We know don't we, Mr Rares?"

Rares nodded as if struck dumb.

"The visit, we're sure, will be linked to Stella's death. You must be aware that with Stella's death we've eliminated one weak link. You were meant to curb her enthusiasm for alcohol and drugs, not deny her, but moderate her intake so that she was controlled. That wasn't the case and now she's gone. With her passing, we've all lost a vital source of income."

Angel watched Rares' head shake and nod as if controlled by strings and in many cases his gestures failed to correspond to the correct responses. He was clearly consumed by fear. They were talking about a girl he had loved as if she were a meal, a takeaway to be discarded when no longer needed. His emotions choked him.

"You know that it doesn't end there, with Stella's death. It can't. What are we to do, Mr Rares if we are to protect our family, our livelihoods?" There was a long pause. "Can you say?"

Rares fidgeted on the chair, chewing his lip until he could taste the metallic bitterness of blood flush his mouth.

"With your permission, I can go back home and work in Romania. I have many skills and I love this family. I'm sorry for the trouble that we have here but it's not all of my doing." His pleading eyes darted back and forth between his two inquisitors.

"Have you been seated in this chair before, Mr Rares, and if so what were you told then?"

"Last chance..." his voice trailed away.

"Sorry I didn't catch that."

"It was the last chance I was told. I've done everything I could, everything I was told to do. Stella was the reason I sat here the first time and she's the reason I sit here now, it is the same crime, I'm being punished twice." His voice rose as his desperation and pleading increased.

Angel looked at his father.

"You're correct Mr Rares, all we require is loyalty. Since that first meeting you've... well, you've demonstrated that or let's say, we hope you have. So providing the police were only paying you a visit to let you know of Stella's death, all will be well." There was a long pause, a pause that seemed to measure a lifetime to Rares. "But I'm afraid that's not the case. We know that the police in white coats came, they came with a sniffer dog and they called at your trailer before breaking down the door. Mr Rares, did you know that they took away things belonging to you? What might those things be?"

Rares chewed his lip with more force, his mind focussed on the steroid bottles he had forgotten to destroy. "I know of nothing. The trailer is clean. They take anything to justify their visit. You know they would just to show their visit was justified. There's nothing!"

No one spoke. The sun appeared again and the needles of light ended at Rares' leg, forming strong, white circles. He felt the sudden warmth.

"If all goes quiet, if we hear nothing, then we don't have a problem," Hai Yau smiled as he finished. "However, if we hear other things, Mr Rares, you know that we have to protect the family. The family, my family is more important than one individual. You'll stay here until things become clearer." They both stood and Rares remained seated, his head bowed.

***

Cyril wiped the sweat from his forehead as his legs and his unoccupied arm moved back and forth. It had to be said that the cross-trainer was his least favourite piece of the gym's torture equipment. Heavy bass music boomed around the building, encouraging greater effort and exercise. The mute television was suspended high in front of him and he read the text. The early morning local news showed a clear photograph of the man wanted by the North Yorkshire Police, the photograph that Cyril had released. Cyril hoped that it would lead to some calls from the public; he knew Rares Negrescu couldn't be far away. Stella's death, he thought, added to the indictment of holding dangerous dogs, might make him desperate enough to flee the country. He stopped exercising and wiped his brow before telephoning Liz.

"Put out a check on all ports and airports for Rares Negrescu, you know the procedure. And Liz, run another check on Stella and see if you can find more on her husband. I think his name was Petev Costin if I remember correctly. I'll be there shortly." Cyril hung up and walked to the changing room. Had he naïvely missed something? If he had, it was very unusual. HOLMES had thrown up the connection of the same name, 'Petev' but that was too obvious and probably coincidental, HOLMES threw up connections like that from the free text database and that is why the good, old, discerning coppers were vital to interpret the plethora of regurgitated information.

Liz lifted the phone and started the procedure for the requested checks to begin, it would mean linking with The National Crime Agency and Border and Transport Police. The system was in place to enable swift implementation. However, she did cynically wonder if they were closing the metaphorical stable door too late.

***

The same television news filled the kitchen of the farmhouse and the displayed photograph could have been nobody but Rares. Angel looked across towards his father and raised one eyebrow before smashing his fist onto the table. The crockery jumped and coffee spilled onto the white cloth.

"My son, if you are patient in one moment of anger, you will escape a hundred days of sorrow." Angel's frown broadened as he thought about what his father had just said. Hai Yau put down his knife and fork before placing his hands by his plate. "We knew this all along. We knew that Rares would need to leave us. We need to follow our ancestors' philosophy and look at the problem and how we're to solve it. When you toss a pebble into the pond you need to see where all of the ripples will end, it is then, and only then, that you know your chosen path. We know what we must do; we know too that it is the right thing to do. Let's talk and toss the pebble together my son. We have many ripples to watch."

***

The phone on the desk rang. Owen was lobbing screwed up paper towards a waste- basket strategically angled across the room; by the number of paper balls surrounding the target he was clearly no great shot. He was taking advantage of the calm before the storm.

"DS Owen." He picked up the receiver, knocking over the tea mug that was balanced on a pile of papers, the brown residue dribbled out bringing with it the remnants of the teabag he thought he had removed.

"Shit! Sorry, not you. I've just… never mind go on."

He listened and jotted down notes on the tea-splattered pad before hanging up. It wasn't what he was expecting. He picked up the tea bag and threw it at the bin and to his surprise it went straight in. A routine enquiry had found one taxi firm that had delivered a young woman to Kettlesing Head lay-by. It was seven months ago but the driver remembered thinking that it was a strange destination until his boss had helped him put two and two together; it was his first week! The woman had been collected on Union Street and had been returned to the same place just before midnight. Owen asked the officer to 'invite' the driver to the station so that he could make a proper identification of Stella from the pictures held.

Owen went to the incident room; it was busy. Within half an hour Rares Negrescu had been spotted at the same time as far afield as Selby, Richmond and sitting on a bench overlooking the half-moon pond at Studley Royal. *'Anyone with a large, brown dog will be reported'*, he thought. Each sighting, however, would be added to the computer and each would be given a unique message number before generating an action that would mean an interview, which in turn would mean more names, more descriptions. It had to be remembered that the one that might seem totally false and far-fetched now with all the conflicting data, might prove to be accurate. You could just never tell.

Owen returned and looked at the input on his computer screen from the DNA database. "Yes! Yes! Yes!" he announced.

Three people looked across, one more inquisitive than the other two.

"Another tea-bag successfully in the bin? Or is it a Lottery win?" Stuart asked.

"Better than that. We ran a speculative search and have a positive on the cigarette butt retrieved from the visit to the caravan."

He suddenly had a warm glow remembering Cyril's words, '*You can't learn to get a gut feeling, you're born with it,*'

He smiled to himself, but the smile didn't last for long.

Chapter Nineteen

Peter slid his hand along Joan's thigh, lifting the hem of her skirt before touching the lace he had so wanted to find. Joan put her hand on his.

"Not here and not now. I've work in fifteen minutes and although I know you usually manage in less time than that, I'd like a little longer!" She moved away and smiled at him. You have some important news for me or I think that's what you said." She opened her bag and took out a tube of mints, popped one in Peter's mouth and then followed suit.

"I'm in Leeds for the weekend, I've some business to attend to and wondered if you'd like a weekend away. You shop whilst I work and then a meal and then..." he ran his hand again up her thigh.

"I'll let you know; as always it depends on my mother's mood. I've told you what she's like."

"Tell her it's linked with work, make something up."

"Lie you mean? Not at my age. It's the truth or nothing. I've done enough lying and covering up to last a life time."

Peter pulled a face. "Something else. I do the accounts for a family who own a few food establishments and they've invited me to the opening of their new restaurant. Unfortunately I can't make it but I thought you might be able to use the invitation as a lever with your mother. The owner is expecting you; the truth is, he looks forward to meeting you. Besides, from what you say, your mother might be useful in the kitchen, if the ovens pack up she could cook the meals by breathing on them!"

Joan slapped him hard on the arm. "One day I might turn into my mother so be warned!" she laughed, opening the car door. "Where is it this restaurant?"

"In Harrogate." Peter leaned over, put his hand in the pocket of his jacket that hung behind the seat. He took out an envelope and handed it to Joan.

"I'll ring you tonight." She blew him a kiss and walked to her car.

***

Peter sat on the sofa, a beer in one hand and a slice of pizza in the other. ACDC blasted from the stereo when his phone rang. It was Joan.

"Nightclub? She giggled.

"Sorry, got a mouthful of Pizza." He leaned for the remote and muted the sound. It was as if he had suddenly gone deaf. "Can you hear me?"

"Yes and it was lovely seeing you at lunchtime." She paused. "Are you sitting down? Good news. It's a yes on two fronts. *We are go for launch*," she announced in an American accent. "*Countdown begins for the weekend* and..." her voice changed back to normal, "mother is agreeable to the new restaurant visit. I nearly died when she eventually said yes. Mind you, life and death decisions have been made in less time!"

***

Rares sat up on hearing the key turn in the lock and his heart beat faster as the hot, prickling sense of fear flushed through his body. It was as if he had stopped breathing. The youth, who had escaped The Darkie, flicked on the light. Rares hoped the choice of messenger wasn't indicative of the next step.

"Some food and a change of clothes." He put the tray on the table and tossed a black plastic bin-bag onto the bed. "Your old clothes are to go in this bag now." He stood and watched Rares remove his clothing. "Shower and put these on before you eat."

Rares stood naked, his hands covering his genitals whilst he stared at the youth who collected the clothes and placed them in the bag. He picked it up and nervously tied a knot in the top. He looked back at Rares and closed the door. Rares' fear increased after seeing the facial expression of the person leaving; he had seen something in

116

his eyes. Rares turned and looked at the clothes that had been left, they were definitely not his. The fear made him vomit.

***

The kitchen at *Zingaro* was busy. Hai Yau had chosen those workers who had demonstrated a definite flair and they were busy with his recipes. He sampled the food during preparation and smiled. Angel watched from the side and was clearly impressed by not only his father's sensitive approach to the staff, but also his energy. He was alive, his face beamed in happiness when a flavour was acceptable. He stopped the group and praised individuals, patting the cook on the back and getting the others to applaud. Angel saw the pleasure on their faces, in some cases, for the first time since their arrival.

"Come, my son. You must try this pasta Sanda's prepared. It's better than mine." His mouth was full of food.

Sanda smiled and blushed.

Angel took a fork and picked pasta from the bowl. "That's excellent." He looked at Sanda, remembering the hayloft. She looked down as if to indicate that she knew just what he was thinking and was trying to flush the thought away. "You've two skills I now compliment you on." His tongue licked his lips. "Well done!"

Angel now started to speak in English with his father, knowing that many of the new kitchen staff would fail to comprehend. "We'll take Rares to The Darkie tonight. We'll use two dogs. Don't worry, there'll be no mistakes this time and we'll clean up better than before."

"Take two new people with you to witness the result of failing my family. Don't let them see where you're taking them. The word will spread quickly. Take one from here, not from the kitchen, from the waiting staff and one other, preferably one of the new working girls. You'll know who's not been as co-operative and profitable as you'd hoped."

Angel immediately looked at Sanda and smiled.

Hai Yau put his mouth near to his son's ear and whispered a name. "Karl, Yes?"

Angel looked puzzled and frowned but nodded his agreement.

Hai Yau clapped his hands. "To work everyone. We have little time."

As Angel left, Sanda's eyes followed him. She had heard the name 'Rares' mentioned and thought of the only man here who had showed her true compassion. She understood the implication of the word dogs; intuitively she knew that it did not bode well.

Angel sat in the car and proudly looked at the Restaurant. They had done well. He removed his mobile from his pocket and dialled.

"I want you here by nine. We need a van and it has to be as planned, white, clean and untraceable. You'll meet in the usual place. I'll not be with you. It has to be perfect this time. I take it Jim was where he said he'd be? Did he take the package and realise the implications of what was said?" There was a pause. "We know just what he is, he'll not return. You did well to walk away. Until later."

Angel hung up then immediately made a second call. He calmly explained his father's request and then listened. "You've no choice in this matter, you're family and we support each other just as we have supported you. A request from my father is really an order. You'll come to the restaurant at seven this evening. Bring some old clothes that will be destroyed afterwards. Don't be late. By the way, did you know that Stella was dead?" Angel listened before answering a stream of questions. "Overdose of some kind. She was tricking in a wagon." Angel moved the phone from his ear for a second but continued to listen. "She'll be adopted at some stage. She's in foster care at the moment. You need to forget her, leave her alone. That will be the best for all, especially her. Are you listening? We'll talk further tonight." Angel hung up. The conversation was over.

***

Cyril looked at the computer screen. He smiled. It was clear that Stuart had stopped chewing his pencil long enough to track down the owner of the Leeds flat and the occupants Peter Anton had shared with whilst at university as Owen had instructed. It was hardly surprising, that considering his temporary work whilst a student, it belonged to a local Chinese businessman.

"Owen!" Cyril bellowed as he continued to read the report. It gave details of the owner and the names of those occupying the flat during Anton's time; there were seven in all. Some had occupied the apartment for only a short period whilst others seemed to have been more permanent, some starting as others finished. According to the report, only two had been interviewed, the others had found employment out of the country on completion of their studies. One of the former group now lived in London and the other in Brighton. Neither had returned to Leeds nor knew the whereabouts of the others.

Cyril scribbled a note and put it in front of an officer who was busily ploughing through a mountain of paper. She smiled at Cyril and picked up the phone, her index finger stabbing in the numbers.

Cyril appeared at the door. "Owen, there doesn't seem to be anything strange about Peter Anton's accommodation whilst at Leeds but I want to talk to him about his past in Romania. Call on him at work. I know it's in Leeds but we need to know what happened in his past and then we can maybe close that door. Take Stuart, he knows about his student past. Try to discover if he's still seeing Joan Baines and if so whether there's any, what shall we say, intimacy?" Cyril smiled and pulled a face.

Owen looked at Cyril remembering his general demeanour on first seeing Joan Baines. He wondered whether the latter part of the questioning was for a more selfish purpose. He knew Cyril could be a bit of a Jack the Lad.

"By the way, I heard about your gut being right with the chap at the caravan. Well done! Always said you were as keen as mustard and made for this job. All we now have to do is develop your dress sense." Cyril smiled.

Owen's jaw dropped. That was the first real compliment, even though it was barbed, that he had heard his boss utter. Either he was improving or Cyril was growing soft. If he were honest, he knew it wasn't the latter.

"Staying there all day basking in the glory of a compliment or do you have an appointment in Leeds?" Cyril spoke without lifting his head.

The officer who had made the call shouted across. "Peter Anton's in the office all afternoon and will be expecting you. Didn't sound too happy though. Wanted to know why you couldn't see him at home."

Cyril just lifted his shoulders, "Beggars can't be choosers, love. It's as simple as that."

***

Peter Anton sat in his office and stared out of the window. The dark grey of the sky certainly matched his demeanour. He was ceasing to be the master of his own destiny. Firstly he had received orders from Angel earlier in the day and then a request from the police. He cursed Drew Sadler under his breath, he cursed his own gambling habit and he cursed Stella. He could have been out of all of this by now, he could have controlled his own gambling but he couldn't control her. Because of her growing demands, he had needed to stay committed to Angel. The one consolation was that he was now free from the ghost of Stella Gornall and he had been grateful to Angel for ensuring that their paths seldom met. The one thing he regretted most of all, however, was the lack of contact with his daughter but that he had to live with. He opened his wallet and took out a photograph of a baby. Just how deeply was he prepared to fall? He walked over to the shredder and switched it on. His daughter's fragmented picture passed before him and fell into the large plastic holding bin. He felt that his life was doing the same. '*Maybe she isn't mine as Angel so often said*', he thought, wrestling with his contorted emotions. Knowing Stella's work, the child could have belonged to any of her many paying punters. How many thought they were fathers? How many were told the sob story to extort some more drugs or cash? He knew he too could be one of the fools. What he did know for certain was that he now had Joan. He smiled for the first time since receiving the telephone call but not for long. Work seemed to drag, as his anxiety at the pending visit increased. He continued to look at the clock but time still seemed to pass so slowly. The phone on his desk rang, startling him.

"Two gentlemen to see you, Mr Anton, they say they have an appointment but it's not in the diary."

"Sorry, my fault. They only rang earlier on my mobile and I just haven't had a moment. Please show them up Sylvia."

"Sorry to trouble you at work but we just have to tie up some loose ends and we'll be out of your hair. This is DC Park." Stuart nodded and took out his note pad. Owen took out the Dictaphone. "Do you mind?"

Peter shook his head. "Will I get copies of these 'informal' chats or do I need a lawyer present?"

"We can move to the station and you're welcome to call a lawyer, you're still under oath. This is as informal as our last meeting but you can stop the conversation whenever you like. As I said, it's purely to tie up some loose ends that have come to our attention from information we have received from the Romanian police."

Peter, assuming it would be about his past, just started to talk. Words came easily and from their response his assumption was proved to be correct. "Prison for the violent attack on one miserable, aggressive bastard who did nothing but beat my mother, get drunk and go with prostitutes leaving little money in a very poor household. I also believe he killed my father but I've no proof, just a gut feeling."

Owen suddenly took more notice, he was very much aware of the accuracy of such anatomical sensations.

Peter paused, looking at both officers after seeing a change in Owen's stance. "You and me both will never understand the phenomenon. I didn't have any firm evidence and yet I instinctively used the hammer. When you see your mother suffering and in so much pain, working all hours to make ends meet, and then this guy staggers in at the end of the day, all the money spent on alcohol and demands food, even demands sex in front of me and then beats us both because there's neither available. It's hard. One day he came home and I was out helping a neighbour fix his boat. When I returned the bastard was raping my mother, yes raping her. Her face was bleeding, her nose was smashed. I just hit him hard with the hammer I was carrying, his own hammer, the one I had been using to help mend the boat. He stopped. I made him stop. I ran back to the neighbours and then everything is a blur. The police and medics came; my mother was just sitting there staring as if in a trance. She never spoke, just stared." He bowed his head and began to weep. "Sorry!"

"It must've been terrible. Can you go on? You mentioned that he'd killed your father. Is that the case?"

"I'll never know the truth but my mother once said to me after one of our beatings that this monster was not always like that. She told me that he was my father's childhood friend but that he'd always been jealous of my father. She said that he told her that he was more of a man than my father who spent too much time reading and thinking and that she should have married him. In 1989, the Romanian people rose up to depose Ceausescu; both he and my father joined the rioting civilians when the army switched allegiance. My father, I was told, was politically strong and wanted the system to change but he had been afraid to voice his views before this time because of the Securitate. Too many people with a small political voice simply disappeared. During the '89 struggle many people were killed, particularly those loyal to Ceausescu but also there were a number of other deaths, civilian deaths from snipers. My father was found dead with a bullet in his back. He had been with my stepfather. Things were calming when he was killed, it was December 23rd, the leaders had fled like cowards but I'm pleased to say, not for long. In two days they were dead; a trial followed by a firing squad. People said that my stepfather saw an opportunity to eliminate the human obstacle that had denied him my mother; getting rid of him then was an opportunity that might never come again. It's strange that nobody else witnessed the death. As you can imagine it caused much gossip, especially when my mother married him. That's why we moved away, moved to Constanța. After prison, I went to University and then came to England to do my MA." He paused and looked at both policemen as if anticipating their next question. "Before you ask, I saved whilst working and received some sponsorship from local businessmen and I'm grateful to them. Times were changing and there was an optimism, a way forward that people had been denied for twenty-five years under Ceausescu."

Stuart was busy scribbling and checking dates mentally. "How long did you spend in prison, Mr Anton?"

"I was fifteen years old when I hit him and I served four years in various institutions. Times were not too bad, it wasn't like the old days but it wasn't pleasant. It was there that I decided to make more of my life, to study like my father. It was then three years at university as I've said."

Owen looked at Stuart who nodded to suggest he had heard enough. "May I now ask you about Joan Baines or Sadler, if you prefer?"

"I need a coffee. You?" He phoned Sylvia with a request. "Sorry, now please ask away."

"I know you supported Joan through a difficult time as well as loaning her money but is there now more to that relationship?"

"I fail to see the relevance other than your wanting to know whether we were having an affair when Drew was alive; that might suggest I had a hand in his downward spiral and possibly his death, after all, I have a record for violence. Well…"

There was a tap on the door and Sylvia entered with the coffee. She handed round the cups and left.

"Where was I?"

"Your relationship with Joan Baines," Stuart answered.

"The answer is simple, we were not then, but are now developing a relationship, I'm pleased to say. That sounded rather clinical but it's not. We're roughly the same age and we like each other's company. I know it's soon after Drew's death but from what I understand their relationship died well before she went to live with her parents. I believe I'm not breaking the law, Sergeant!"

"Thanks for being so candid, Mr Anton. I think that's everything. Again we're sorry for disturbing you at work."

By four they were back at the station. Stuart would up-load the interview and Owen went to check his desk. There was a note from Cyril.

There's no reference to the buccal swab taken from Peter Anton. Why not?

Owen sat and put his head in his hands. "Bugger!"

Chapter Twenty

If Owen heard someone utter 'DNA' again, he would scream. He hoped it would not be mentioned at this juncture whilst he was explaining his perceptions of Peter Anton's interview to Cyril.

"He's had it tough and he appears to be trying to build a better life. His stepfather sounded a right bastard."

"Owen, nobody deserves an attack resulting in permanent brain damage, no matter how evil they are, although I must say that I had to put my stick away before I saw you today. I've only one word to say and that's swab."

Cyril looked Owen directly in the eye as he said it.

"I forgot! In all the dashing about, I made an error. And for the record it was a hammer."

"I know it was a bloody hammer! You forgot! What do you mean you forgot?" Cyril looked directly at Owen. "You simply had to ask for his co-operation. The way things are, he would have been more than willing. His DNA would confirm if there's a connection between him and Stella. Her first husband was a Petev…"

Cyril noted the sceptical look on Owen's face as if fully aware that he was clutching at straws, and thin ones at that, but he continued to make his point.

"And I know the age difference is enormous and that there are hundreds of bloody Petevs but for one buccal swab it was worth seeing if Christina is his."

"About eleven years, Sir." Owen confirmed stifling a yawn.

"What is?

"Their age difference. That's not massive. It's plausible. I'll call and see him. I'll need a nurse with me to do the test. I'm sorry." '*From hero to zero in one day*', he thought to himself. He turned towards the door about to leave; he felt like kicking something and Cyril was closest. He suddenly fired another volley.

"And whilst we're on the subject, your speculative DNA test on the cig butt hasn't brought a name. Found in two historical rape cases. One in Ripon three years ago and one in Leeds last year. No arrest. Take a look at the bottom of that sheet."

Owen looked up, his face showing his disbelief. "Christina? Our Christina? Stella's child?"

"It doesn't lie, Owen. Add your description of the man to both cases and see if anything gets churned out."

"It's done, Sir. The guy would stand out in a crowd what with his height, his squashed nose and sporting only one and a half ears. Mind you, there's no guarantee he had any of these distinguishing features apart from his height when he committed the crimes."

He turned and walked towards the door, shaking his head.

"Is that it, Sir? I've a mountain of paperwork."

Cyril looked at Owen. "We need luck like this. Well done!" The telephone rang.

"Bennett." The tone of his voice made the caller pause momentarily. "Bennett" He repeated.

Cyril listened, his face contorted into a frown. "One second." He covered the mouthpiece and called for Owen who appeared again but this time looking even more frustrated. Cyril put the phone on speaker.

"It's unlikely he'll pull through, major head trauma and in intensive care. Found at about 15:30 yesterday within a stone's throw of a bar in Newcastle. Nothing seems to have been taken. Tracked him to your investigation once it was entered onto the system. Thought you'd like the heads up immediately. We have someone at the hospital 24/7 if he should wake."

Cyril could see Owen frowning and mouthing the words, 'Who?'

"It's the driver, James Nolan."

Cyril thanked the caller after jotting down the name and rather abruptly, ended the telephone conversation.

"We need to get CCTV footage from the bus station both here and in Newcastle as well as streets in the locality. Also ANPR records for routes from the station out in the direction of Newcastle and routes into the Newcastle bus station area. The National Express goes through Newcastle on its way to Edinburgh. Is that coincidence or accident? And Owen, get someone to check the records for the coach. The video should give us some clues. We'll see when our man got on and off. There should be names and addresses of other passengers who booked on line."

Cyril's hand reached out and picked up his electronic cigarette before turning it in his fingers. Owen looked at his face and could clearly see the thought processes at work.

***

The taxi pulled up outside the gate of what was a row of Victorian stone houses that had been converted into apartments. Cyril jumped out, walked up the short path before checking the numbers on the illuminated intercom. He noted that he wanted Apartment 2. He pressed the intercom before turning to look at the view from the doorway. Beyond the taxi stood The Stray, The slight hum of traffic could be heard but the sound of a blackbird hidden high in some far-off foliage was the dominant noise until someone knocked loudly on a window. He turned to look. Dr Julie Pritchett stood by the bay window, holding a hairbrush in one hand and proffering two fingers with the other. Fortunately for Cyril, their position suggested that she would be only two minutes and he smiled. He turned back to search out the blackbird. He failed to locate it even though it sounded so close.

Julie appeared dressed in a blue trouser suit and looking radiant.

"Your carriage awaits M'lady," he said in an exaggerated Yorkshire accent. "You're looking truly elegant Ms Pritchett."

Cyril paused and looked back at the apartment. "Rather lovely looking pad too if I may be so bold."

"Sorry I'm a little late but…you know what I'm going to say. Thank you, yes. Not bad for a quick turn around and yes the apartment is lovely. I was unsure at first but its proximity to town is just perfect, but if we're talking of uncertainty, I take it you're not too happy about this restaurant, Cyril?"

Cyril held the door and she climbed into the taxi. He quickly checked the road and nipped round the other side.

"Italian, Chinese, Romanian! Would you be confident? I believe the owner's only really had take away establishments before but I could be wrong on that score, as I know little about the guy. We'll see and as my mother always said, bless her, '*The proof of the pudding is in the eating!*' Besides, he's a brave man committing the money to the project and believe me it can't have been cheap!"

Angel greeted Cyril as he entered the restaurant. "Thank you so much for coming. As you can see we're filling up."

Cyril looked round quickly trying to identify any familiar faces. With only a cursory glance, he recognised no one.

"May I introduce Dr Pritchett? This young man is the son of the owner. Angel, is that correct?"

"Yes, only things missing are my wings. I had those clipped by my father long ago," he laughed. He leaned over and shook her hand. "A pleasure to welcome you Doctor. Please let me show you to your table, then I'll leave you to have a look around. Hopefully you'll not find too many…" he paused and smiled at the couple, "teething troubles tonight!"

Cyril smiled remembering their previous conversation before complimenting Angel on the restaurant's ambience; the lighting, the flowers and the impeccable waiting staff certainly reflected an expensive commitment to success.

"Tonight will be a full tasting menu of which my father and his team are very proud. My father will talk with everyone after the meal. He's too excited and a little nervous right now. If there's anything you need, anything at all, please see me, or one of my staff. Your complimentary drinks are here."

A waiter smiled and proffered a tray containing flutes of Champagne and glasses of orange juice.

Cyril ignored the orange juice. "Cheers!"

"May these be the worst of our days, Cyril," Julie said before touching Cyril's glass with hers. "Thanks for the invitation. I can't remember the last time I ventured out socially mid..." She paused, not completing the sentence as Cyril had been distracted by the entrance of two more guests, both women. One was about thirty, attractive and elegantly dressed, whilst the other was older with the appearance, to the casual observer, of a dreadnought. *It could be her mother*, she thought. "I've worked on corpses with a happier countenance. Old conquests?"

Cyril laughed. "No! I'm dreadfully sorry but I know those ladies, professionally I hasten to add. One I can see coming here tonight and enjoying the evening but the other!" He sipped his drink and looked back at Julie.

"The older one will be dancing on the table with her knickers on her head by nine," she whispered.

Cyril nearly choked on his Champagne. He had clearly underestimated the good Doctor and he knew he had made a wise decision to spend the evening with her.

"That, my dear, is the wife and mother-in law of the bag of bits you collected from Pannal Road." It was Julie's turn to choke on her Champagne. "I think I mentioned that they'd had a rocky final year or two. Well, the one on the right could just have had something to do with that."

"She could certainly guard a hen house!" Julie observed.

"She could guard a high security prison!"

The evening was not only relaxing but the food was proving to be excellent.

A small sorbet arrived with what looked like a miniature window garden decorating the edge. Cyril turned to look at one of the paintings on the wall that Julie was discussing when he saw

Mrs Baines stand before receiving directions from a waitress. She was heading towards the toilets. He then realised that Joan was moving across the room towards them.

"DCI Bennett, how lovely to see you! Are you enjoying the meal?"

Cyril introduced Julie and exchanged the usual pleasantries when he caught sight of Mrs Baines in his peripheral vision. She looked anxious and more than a little flustered. He turned his head and Joan instinctively registered Cyril's changed expression and followed his gaze.

"Please excuse me, something hasn't pleased her, probably the quality of the toilet paper." She giggled but it didn't conceal her frustration. "Lovely to meet you both. Duty calls, I must go and calm troubled waters."

"Good luck" Cyril proffered before looking back at Julie but he could see that the mother-daughter discussion fascinated her. Within minutes both were leaving the restaurant.

"I guess the knickers will not be her crown tonight." Julie chuckled. "I'd better go and check that all's up to scratch in the ladies. Something's truly rattled her cage. Maybe she forgot to put any knickers on this evening and she's realised her cabaret performance is ruined."

Cyril laughed out loud and a number of faces turned in his direction. He took the opportunity to go to the bar; he needed to stretch his legs. Cyril refused the complimentary Champagne after the first glass; he particularly fancied the Italian beer. Whilst he was standing at the bar, he noticed two men walk briskly across the car park from the rear of the building and climb into what looked like a large van, Cyril checked his watch, it was five past nine; he shook it just to be on the safe side. He noted that one of the men was considerably taller than the other. Another car pulled in to the car park. Another figure emerged. Even in the dark Cyril could tell that it was Angel, running from the rear of the restaurant and leaning on the van's window. He also noted that the driver of the car transferred to the waiting van before it left. Angel's arms flailed as if he were upset over something. As he turned to collect his drinks from the bar he couldn't fail to see that the kitchen door leading to the restaurant was held ajar; a waiter was calling for a missing order. Cyril's eyes fell on one of the staff, a female, who seemed dreadfully upset as she stared out onto the parked cars. He turned back to see what she might be looking at but all he observed was the van leaving and Angel's return.

"Will there be anything else, Sir?" the barman requested.

Cyril turned away from the window, smiled and shook his head. He paid and returned to his table arriving just before Julie. Julie just raised her eyebrows and shook her head. "Given them a thorough inspection and all appears in order."

***

Cezar pulled the white van onto a deserted road and then attached fluorescent magnetic blue and yellow reflective strips to the rear doors and to each side. He added lights to the roof giving the van the appearance of belonging to the police, although no wording had been applied. The orange glow from the streetlights barely crept through the darkened windows in the rear doors. Rares tugged at the electrical ties binding his hands and feet as the two caged dogs squealed in anticipation, eager to get at the trussed body. One of the two men in the back kicked the cage and laughed whilst the other just stared at Rares.

Once ready the van moved off. Within fifteen minutes it was turning on to Fallow Road. Cezar parked up and the two people in the back cut the electrical ties from around Rares' ankles and took him from the van. They quickly bundled him over the small fence and into the undergrowth. The gag in his mouth made breathing difficult and his bound arms meant that he had to rely on his captives' support on the dark, sloping ground. Cezar looked up the road and noticed another car appear. The driver flashed his lights before parking a short distance away. Three people emerged, two looking more than a little bewildered. Cezar checked that they were wearing gloves. They followed the first group over the fence with a great deal of apprehension before blindfolds were tied. Nobody spoke. Cezar again scanned the road and collected a box and a stun baton, which he attached to his belt from the back. Quickly he collected the muzzled dogs and followed the others, cursing as the dogs tangled themselves in the fence. Subtly, he belted both of them to sort the problem. The additional gloom from the overhanging trees and the steep slope made walking particularly difficult, especially with the dogs, but Cezar's strength kept the dogs close by. It was a little easier once the ground had levelled where the railway track had once run. They were soon at the entrance to the tunnel, its arched opening partly camouflaged by the hanging ivy. The metal tracks and wooden sleepers had been removed years ago. A small stream of rust-coloured water dribbled out at the bottom before disappearing sideways into the brambles.

Cezar handed out the head torches. Little was said and when it was, it was in Romanian. Cezar turned on his head torch; the others would only be illuminated once in the tunnel. There was no need to draw unnecessary attention to the dark siding.

Discarded beer cans and bottles littered the place and smashed glass glowed almost jewel-like in the grass as the light was reflected. Part of a bicycle lay almost concealed, the green arms of brambles locking it in a final embrace.

Harrogate's Brunswick Tunnel was built in 1848 to allow trains to run into the centre of Harrogate without the polluting smoke. However, its life was short-lived being made redundant fourteen years later. It had a reprieve during the Second World War when it was used as an air-raid shelter. Bombproof walls and toilets were constructed, these, however, were now heavily disfigured through time, vandalism and graffiti. Steps were constructed to ease access and at one time the way emerged somewhere near Leeds Road, an entrance that is now permanently closed and concealed. To a generation of children, it had become known as The Darkie.

Cezar was the last to move through the opened grill that normally blocked the path to the only remaining entrance. Those already in, stood silently, blindfolds removed. The four hundred yard tunnel yawned ahead. At the far end, looking smaller than they actually were stood the multi-coloured, brick walls that showed the true perspective of the tunnel's length. Water-filled corrugations ran across the dirt floor, permanent scars made by the long-removed railway sleepers. Their flat, puddled surfaces reflected some of the light onto the arched, stone roof. The echoing sounds of dripping water and muzzled, excited dogs added to the tension felt by all.

Rares knew what was coming as his eyes looked for the space that had once been occupied by the unfortunate tramp, but he could see that it was empty apart from some remnants of discarded clothes. Unfortunately for him, lightning did not strike the same spot twice! His eyes ran the length of the tunnel as eager hands forced him onto the floor before stripping the clothes from his body.

Cezar brought out the staple gun and one of the men holding Rares by the arm instinctively moved his head. He had been there before and he had felt the pain and fear. Rough hands pulled the elastic over Rares' head and he felt the sharp, intense pain of the first staple bite through the skin on his forehead and splay against bone. With his mouth blocked, snot and saliva erupted from his nostrils as another and then another staple stitched the torch's elastic to his head.

"You know the rules?" Cezar turned to the two frightened and confused family members who had been brought down to witness the event. "A lesson to you all. This is what happens to those who show disloyalty to the family. Watch and learn."

The girl, on seeing the man being stripped, grew even more anxious, knowing that she had not been fully co-operative. She anticipated his rape or hers to follow and then she looked at the dogs. She blocked her imagination; surely they would not use them for that purpose? She shivered. Peter Anton, standing between them, felt her body shaking and tried to calm her but his efforts had little effect.

***

Cyril and Julie were eventually introduced to Hai Yau who seemed more than thrilled with the evening. Everyone applauded as he brought out the kitchen staff. Cyril was surprised at the number. His eyes scanned for the girl he had seen earlier but she was not amongst them. He looked at Julie.

"Strange that," he said in a low voice. His eyes darted around the room, thinking that she might have come into the restaurant earlier but he could not see her.

"What is?"

"I know one of the kitchen staff is missing. I saw her earlier and she looked very upset."

"Probably over-egged the pudding and got a clip round the ear."

"Very true, they were probably all on edge. Are you ready?"

Cyril took another look round before making his way to the bar as they were leaving in the hope of seeing her in the kitchen. She was nowhere to be seen. Angel appeared with a smile.

"I have to say that the restaurant and the meal did you credit. Everything has been perfect. I noticed two ladies leave before the final courses, I hope nothing was wrong?"

"The policeman in you is showing, Mr Bennett. No, nothing was wrong. I think the elderly lady found it all a little too exciting, either that or she had too much Champagne!" Angel smiled and shook Cyril's hand. He looked down and noticed a twenty-pound note had been subtly transferred in the action.

"For the staff," said Cyril. "I'm sure it's been a traumatic experience for many, especially those in the kitchen, first night nerves and all!" He looked over Angel's shoulder towards the kitchen for one last check for the girl but she wasn't there.

"That's very generous. Thank you. Is something wrong?"

"No, sorry."

"Dr Pritchett it has been a pleasure. May I?" he leaned across and kissed her on both cheeks. "Let's hope we see you at *Zingaro* again soon.

He turned to Cyril and their eyes met, each man trying to read what might lay hidden.

***

The ties were cut from Rares' hands. "You know The Chase? Now we'll remove the gag and it's game on for you. If you win, then all's fine, but if not…"

"Please, I've done nothing, I don't deserve this. I'm loyal. They are my dogs."

He started to cry and urine splashed and then dribbled down his legs, it was an involuntary action that had no effect. Cezar jumped back but still managed to slap Rares' head. "Fucking hell!"

Rares could not feel the cold, the wet nor the sharp stones on the soles of his feet, he simply began to run. The light beams followed him, penetrating the gloom of the tunnel like beacons of hope. Rares looked and saw the white stalactites hanging from the roof and his mind filled with the vision of long, sharp, white teeth that he knew would soon follow. It was then that he heard the instruction to release the dogs. He tried to run faster but his feet slid in the oozing mud.

***

The taxi pulled up outside Julie's apartment. "Coffee, DCI Bennett, or do you have other plans?" She slipped her hand onto his. "There might be a little nightcap on offer too!" She smiled and opened the taxi door. Cyril paid and followed her up the path. The entrance hall was as elegant as he had expected from the building's façade. Black and white marble squares stretched the whole length; small, delicate side tables clung closely to the walls, each displaying an ornament or vase of fresh flowers.

"Communal entrance, Cyril. We share it. If you look at the stained glass on the first landing you can see why I'm so enchanted by this place."

She did not see his corrected frown; he knew what communal meant! Had it been anyone else… He climbed the stairs and looked at the large window. Only the streetlight entered through the coloured glass, failing to do justice to the craftsmanship. Leaded-edged, delicate glass flowers framed the internal pattern of what looked like geometric, glass shapes made up of blues and purples. On a summer's day the light show would be magnificent.

"It's fabulous, Julie. Must see it in daylight."

She did not hear, she had moved inside the apartment.

***

The light show in Brunswick Tunnel was anything but magnificent it was clinical and cold. Beams of white from turning heads created sinister patterns on the rough-faced stone blocks that lined the walls. The observers' breath billowed like small vents adding a sinister appearance to the whole macabre scene. For Rares, time seemed to slow as his senses grew, heightened through intense fear. His ears were alert to the sounds behind and he felt no strain from his pumping limbs as he sprinted for life itself. He never flinched as his left big toe was nearly severed on a broken bottle. Held only by the upper flesh, it began to flap as he ran, spewing blood to mix with the mud and the puddles. He was purely focussed on the wall at the far end, a wall that, thankfully, appeared to be increasing in size. He had to reach the safety and security that it represented.

A routine police patrol vehicle ambled down Langcliffe Avenue, the road that was constructed directly above Brunswick Tunnel. All, as usual, was quiet. There had been a number of calls made to the police during the school holidays, reports of youths disturbing the neighbourhood. The local police often found them near the Tunnel's entrance, usually in possession of illicit alcohol, but they never proved to be a problem and were soon disbanded. Now it had been made a regular route for the area police patrol. The Council too had acted by securing the entrance but Cezar had removed part of the metal grill earlier in the day. He would secure it the next day, dressed as a council workman so as not to draw any attention to himself.

The police car slowed and PC Leach glanced down Fallow Road. He noticed the police van. Surely the kids were not there tonight, he had not had a call. He drove on before stopping at the bridge that crossed the railway line linking Harrogate and Leeds. He climbed out and stretched before moving to lean over the parapet. He stared in the direction of the disused Brunswick

Tunnel siding. Trying to penetrate the dark, he could only see the broken, orange glow of the streetlights through the trees that ran along Fallow Road. There was nothing below where the siding ran to the tunnel's entrance. Briefly, he looked across to the other side and as he turned back, it was then that he saw the first, faint flash of a white light. He concentrated his stare on the dense foliage some distance from the track where he had seen the light.

**

Cyril followed Julie into the apartment. She had already selected music and set the mood with the lighting.

"There's some rather nice whiskey in the cabinet under the bookcases, glasses are out, as is some ice!" she called from some far-off room.

Cyril smiled like a cat that had just found the cream. A bottle of Jameson Irish Signature Reserve was still sitting in its cylindrical tube. He quickly poured two measures. He casually allowed his hand to slip, as he poured the whiskey into Julie's glass, after all, it was hers.

"That was a lovely evening, Cyril, and apart from the drinks it was complimentary?" Cyril nodded. "And for a Yorkshireman, evenings don't get better than that, do they?"

"Don't rightly know, but a free Jameson's comes a close second!"

Julie pulled a face. Cyril leaned over and kissed her.

"Now that's better, DCI Bennett."

Cyril took out his mobile and set it to mute. Julie smiled. "See why you're a cop, quick as a flash, Flash." She returned the kiss.

**

PC Leach saw the light for the second time and believed that his colleagues were down at the tunnel entrance. He decided to investigate. He parked close to the van, climbed the fence and using his torch to highlight the path, walked through the bushes and undergrowth. He stopped. The fact was that he had drunk three mugs of coffee before starting his shift. He stood and relieved himself. All was quiet.

Rares jumped, his fingers grasping the top of the brick wall. If he could get his body on the top he was safe. His feet scrambled trying to find purchase but the mud made it impossible against the smooth brick. He jumped again. He felt his strength return as the dogs grew ever closer and he began to scale the wall. The leading dog leap instinctively and its teeth found Rares' left calf. It immediately began shaking its head, tearing muscle and flesh. Rares screamed and kicked the dog frantically with his right foot whilst clinging precariously to the top with his fingers. To his astonishment, he managed to break free. He scrambled to the top of the wall and breathed deeply, he felt neither pain nor elation. The muted dogs squealed as they ran and leapt. Rares raised his arms, he had succeeded, he had done it. One of the spectators raised his arms too, amazed at Rares' speed and agility in climbing the wall with a dog attached to his leg.

Rares leaned back as if trying to get more air into his lungs. Suddenly, he felt his weight shift, he was out of balance and he was going backwards. His feet moved away from the wall. Desperately he started to windmill his arms, trying to bring his weight back above the narrow top of the wall, but it was not enough.

Rares knew he was toppling backwards. He stopped the rotation of his arms and grasped desperately at the rough bricks. Sensing their advantage, the dogs jumped through a gap where a door had once been and then back, unsure of their quarry's position. They would not wait long. Rares began to rock backwards. His feet flicked quickly upwards and he started to fall over the wall, out of sight of those four hundred yards away. The light from his head torch was the only sign of his position until a shrill scream erupted from his throat and the dogs' excitement reached fever pitch. Each leapt at the falling, flailing man, ripping and tearing. The intense screams that now reverberated were amplified in the confined space of the tunnel, only to be echoed by the scream from the girl who was now held firmly by Peter. Neither noise lasted long. The two men raced to get the dogs.

PC Leach heard the scream too. Its whereabouts could not be pinpointed but it made the hair on his neck stand out. He zipped his fly, unfinished. The trickle of warm urine ran down his left leg as he hurriedly made his way to the tunnel entrance. It was then that he saw the people emerging, the lights dancing on the leaves, never appearing to stay in any spot for long. He shone his torch expecting to see his colleagues. Cezar spotted him, the reflection from his police jacket made him easily identifiable. He instinctively grabbed the muzzle he had just fitted to the dog and removed it before slipping its lead. The dog did not hesitate. PC Leach was just about to make the call when the dog hit him hard knocking him off his feet. He tumbled a little down the slope; brambles tangled and scratched his hands. He put his arms up to protect his face from the dog, his screams now filling the valley floor. Cezar approached the melee. Removing the stun baton from his belt, he placed it onto the policeman's neck and pulled the trigger. The dog jumped back as the prostrate figure jerked and then writhed with the shock, entangling himself more in the brambles. Cezar slipped on the muzzle, then attached the lead to the harness.

He turned to the figures standing a few yards away. "Go now!" he called.

"What about Rares?"

"Leave, now!"

The others made their way to the vehicles. Cezar looked down at the officer before smashing his fist into the centre of the policeman's face. His nose exploded. He took the radio and his mobile phone and tossed them into the undergrowth and left, the dog still eager to attack the writhing figure.

"I just hate fucking coppers," he grumbled as he moved up the slope to meet the others. He was neither unflustered and unmoved by his aggression, nor by the night's activity.

***

Cyril checked his watch. It was 5am. He slipped out of the bed. Julie turned but then was still. He dressed and wrote a note before closing the front door. The morning was fine. A slight breeze moved the leaves and the birds were already singing. The dawn had not yet cracked the night sky. He inhaled deeply.

It would take him twenty minutes to walk home; he would shower, breakfast and then head for work. He removed his phone. He had five missed calls, all from Owen.

He returned the call. "Owen what's the urgency?"

"We've located Negrescu. It's not pretty."

"Send a car. I'm on Knaresborough Road just approaching The Empress roundabout."

Within minutes Owen's BMW pulled up alongside Cyril.

"Jesus, it's dreadful. Looks like he's been torn apart by dogs, not pretty. Not pretty at all."

"A modern day Actaeon, that's what we have from the sound of it," Cyril said as he drew on his electronic cigarette and exhaled. "And I bet he wasn't watching Diana bathe."

Owen looked across, confused, but said nothing. He did wonder if the alcohol of the previous evening was still in evidence. PC Leach's car was where it had been parked. Two police vehicles were parked diagonally, blocking the road. Police tape glowed in the blue hue cast by the flashing lights corralling different official vans.

"PC attacked after seeing or hearing a disturbance. From what he's been able to say, and that's not much, poor bastard, he went to see if his colleagues were OK after hearing screams but we didn't have a police presence in this area other than his patrol. We received no calls."

"How is he?"

"He's in a bad way. Bites to the hands and arms. He was hit by what we think was some sort of stun gun by the marks to the left side of his neck and then they literally smashed his face in. It was only when he failed to return calls that he was eventually located. Whoever did this was thorough, they'd even removed his means of communication. He could have died there, he could have choked on his own blood and vomit. It was later that they found Negrescu."

Owen passed Cyril some wellington boots, a high-visibility jacket, gloves and a torch.

"We're to use the railway line, forensics want that trampled area left alone. We can't enter the tunnel either but we have a camera set up."

Lights had been brought in to illuminate the tunnel entrance. Tape marked the area where PC Leach had been found and a small safe area had been established. It was here that a Crime Scene Officer passed Cyril an iPad and uttered a cheery good morning. Cyril put on his reading glasses and stared at the screen, trying to convince himself that the images he was staring at were that of a human being; the torso was very badly deformed and damaged and the skin seemed incredibly white.

"The intense light is giving a false impression, Sir. It appears that the person bled out there. We're bringing in a secondary investigation team to check the whole tunnel. The pathways and this area will be finger searched as soon as we have adequate light."

Cyril was still turning the iPad round in his hand as if searching for the best angle at which to see the facial features. "We sure it's Negrescu?"

"He managed to protect his face and from what the pathologist has reported so far, the attack was not sustained. Leg arteries were torn, there's substantial damage to the genital area and the neck but the victim managed to protect his facial features. It would have been a painful death."

"That confirms it, Owen. There, look! Remember the snake tattoo that ran from behind each ear. That looks very much like it. It's our man."

"So is he Action Man and if so who's Diana, Sir?"

Cyril turned, looked at Owen, whose face was predominantly lit by the light of the iPad screen and simply shook his head. "Sometimes, Owen, I wonder where your classical education is hiding or whether it exists at all!"

"Prefer Pop to Classical. Never been into that morbid instrumental stuff. Give me a good vocal any day of the week. Brian Johnson and ACDC and then you're ready to move!" He smiled at Cyril.

It was at moments like this that Cyril truly wondered if Owen were taking the proverbial and was just toying with him.

"Who's the pathologist?"

"Dr Samual, Dr Pritchett must be busy."

Cyril felt Owen's direct stare and he sensed the smile on his lips. To Cyril's utter relief, Owen's phone rang.

"They've found a van burning in a field off Haggs Road. Fire services are present but there'll be little left."

"Get Forensics there too, there's likely a connection and then take me home. I'll see you in my office at…" Cyril checked his watch, "eight. Get copies of all of this footage."

"It's all uploaded, Sir. Travels through the ether and lands in our system instantaneously. Just like magic or Star Wars."

"If you say so, Owen, but I feel sure that Satan has a finger somewhere in this technology."

He looked at the lights and the white-suited figures. The sky was turning deep red and streaks of orange-yellow began to break down the gloom like hot fingers but light had failed to penetrate the railway cutting.

"And if you must know, I feel as though I'm standing just above Hades down here as it is. Take me home. By the way, the chap you suspected at the caravan, the one with only part of an ear, how tall did you say he was in the report?"

"Six-four to six-six. Taller than me."

Chapter Twenty One

"You did as I said? Everything?"

Cezar nodded as he ate the bread and cheese that filled the plate in front of him. "We'd prepared the van before hand and there was enough fuel to incinerate everything. The dogs actually barked briefly and I've never heard them bark before. I don't know what Rares did to them to make them mute, it must have been one of his special tricks. Poor bastard nearly made it too, got to the wall and managed to scramble up with a dog attached to one of his legs for a while but then the silly sod over balanced and went backwards, arse over tit as fast as that!" He clicked his fingers and laughed. "And that was the end." He chewed another lump of bread.

The words Angel heard were surprisingly poignant. '*The silly sod over-balanced…*' Angel was suddenly reminiscing; he was back on a tree branch in some far off, distant place that was now a lifetime away. He was young and happy, he was reaching for his lost kite that seemed to be smiling back at him, almost mockingly, willing him on to succeed or fall. He could still sense the rough bark on his thighs and the sensation of the coarse string on the tips of his small fingers and then the sudden grip of fear churn inside as he had begun to fall.

"Are you alright? You've gone pale?" Cezar looked unusually concerned.

Angel rubbed his eyes. He could still see the blood on Cezar's hands and under his fingernails from either the dogs or the policeman.

"Yes, I'm fine, just tired. When did the copper arrive?"

"Fuck me, of all the places to appear! He was just coming down the slope as I emerged from the tunnel with one of the dogs. In the torchlight his jacket lit up like a beacon, it even announced that he was a copper. My head torch had hit him smack in the eyes and I knew he could see nothing. Within seconds the dog had him down on the ground and as he rolled he became entangled in brambles and dog's teeth. Before he could recover, I zapped him. Christ he nearly came a foot off the bloody floor and it frightened the crap out of the dog. I don't think he'll be having a conversation anytime soon when you think how hard I hit him. I'd have killed the bastard but I know your rules on that score. I was just pleased he was alone." He ate some more. "He'll think twice about going into dark places alone." Cezar laughed.

Angel could see the partially masticated food in his gaping mouth and quickly looked away.

"My father's still at the restaurant and he mustn't hear this news today. The girl's here? And Karl?"

"He too is here and he'll be fine." Cezar began rolling a cigarette. "I'll have to talk to him and then return him to the restaurant in a couple of days when he's calmed down and had time to put things into perspective. The threat of harm for carelessness must spread. Their understanding that we do not tolerate disloyalty of any kind is critical to keep things as they are."

"The other dogs go too, kill them and then drop them in the old septic tank behind the barn. It's seldom used now that the new septic tank system has been constructed. They'll rot down quickly. Clear all the dog equipment and get Karl and some others to clean the barn. The girl can help too, might take her mind off things." He paused and looked in the gilt-framed mirror that was positioned over the fireplace. "I might help there too. Make sure she's cleaned up. Send her here in an hour, I need to relax a little."

The local television news continued to report only that there had been a police incident and that road closures in the area had been put in place until further notice There would also be delays to the trains between Leeds and Harrogate for the foreseeable future but a bus service was running from Harrogate Station to Pannal. Most people would assume that there had been a fatality on the railway.

***

144

Cyril sat in the incident room and there was a buzz. Liz Graydon was seated opposite him and put down her mug of coffee. She lazily stirred the dark contents, the sound of the spoon being heard above the drone of working chatter.

She looked up at Cyril and smiled. "Every cloud…I was talking with Christina's foster carer and it looks like they've found a placement. The little lady will eventually have some stability in her life."

"Don't forget the biological father is still out there somewhere but I doubt whether it'll affect the placement."

"Don't forget his human rights, Sir. He might play that politically sensitive card if he needs to."

"Only if he knows he's fathered a child. Somehow, from the way he conducts himself, I doubt it."

"I see that they've found evidence that the tunnel was where Drew Sadler met his end. I can't see the connection between Negrescu and Drew Sadler unless the former was in debt too."

"He wasn't, Liz. I don't think that there's a connection at all other than place and manner of death. It is, however, something you said right after Sadler's death. I made a note." He found it before reading it out loud.

'*Someone has used our man as an example. The attack was probably videoed and will be used to deter others from some activity, whether it be falling into debt or some other form of intimidation.*'

"I actually think that you hit the nail nearly on the head. I don't think either was videoed, too risky, but I do think it was a spectator sport, a spectator sport for a macabre reason. It was either a teaching exercise or about gambling. Forensics suggests that there were quite a few people present, that there were two large sized dogs. They've also found two used staples in an area where someone was prostrate whilst they struggled. Rares Negrescu was found with a head torch stapled to his skull." Cyril showed Liz an image of the body. "One man was barefoot so as you can see, we must assume him to be Negrescu as he was naked when found."

"I can't see gambling, Sir, as the odds were so heavily stacked against the runner. Four hundred yards, bare foot, possibly injured, two fast dogs. No, that's a lose, lose scenario."

"What if the stakes were ridiculous? Let's say for argument's sake, a hundred to one with a minimum stake each of £10,000? Four punters at £10,000 is a cool profit of £40,000 for an hour's work. Better than dealing in drugs. What if Negrescu was fit enough to do the run? What if the odds were increased for him to run bare foot and naked? What if they were Negrescu's dogs and he knew he was safe if they were to catch up with him? What if he had practised the run many times and they knew just when to release the dogs so that he would succeed? What if the stapling was for credibility? Now we're stacking the odds in favour of Negrescu. Liz, what if Sadler had been offered the same run to free himself from all of his debts and possibly make a few quid? To set himself free?"

"Or it could be a massive loss, not win. Would you do that, Sir?"

Cyril shook his head. "I don't do hypothetical but I do know desperate people who would though."

"The evidence will come, a shoe print, a finger print, something," Liz said optimistically.

Cyril felt his mobile vibrate before it rang. He took it from his pocket and checked the screen identifying Julie.

"You're an early bird. Where's my breakfast in bed, Cyril Bennett?"

"Julie, yes, sorry. We have a serious incident. Any chance you can pop in? It's urgent. Thanks, see you then."

"Liz, do you remember something Owen came up with about dog attacks? He said that they attacked if a person was compromised by ability or physical condition. We know that Sadler was probably drug ged, drunk or both and we await the toxicology results for Negrescu. He also said that if the dogs were mismanaged or treated cruelly, then that would encourage an attack. I can think of nothing more cruel that keeping dogs to fight and attack, starve them and pump them full of steroids."

Liz moved away and checked the incoming information on the computer next to Cyril's desk. The CCTV footage of the Newcastle attack was available. She ran it. The images were grainy and seemed to come in unnatural bursts, but it clearly showed the victim walking away from the camera. The street was cobbled and fairly narrow with no pavements. She flinched as a van suddenly appeared from the edge of the screen before running into the back of the victim, knocking him to the ground. The driver got out, walked round the front and hit the victim with what looked like a truncheon or a bar. The van then reversed. She played it backwards and then forwards at half speed. Cyril came over.

"Jim Nolan's incident."

Cyril watched. "What do you notice?"

Liz looked carefully again. "He's carrying a bag and when the vehicle leaves it's no longer there. There's no registration number visible on the rear of the van and no reversing light."

"Good, I got two of those but didn't spot the third. I did see, I think, the driver collect the bag."

"Years of finding Wally as a kid!" she said, smiling at Cyril. She ran the video again and paused it. "There, Sir. Yes he's definitely picked up the bag."

"So, no road rage incident? Do we have anything from the Harrogate cameras?"

Liz scrolled through. "A second."

"There's our man. He's holding something but not the same bag, it looks too small. Who's this? Pause it Liz. How tall is he?"

"Couldn't say, there's nothing to measure him against. He's a big fella, mind. What's he doing? Looks like he's taking a photograph of Jim. Can't see his face for the cap."

She pressed play. Cyril and Liz looked at each other as they saw him pass a carrier bag over. It was clear from Jim's gestures that he was not too happy. A bus passed between them and the camera.

"Typical. I'll get someone to check other CCTV in the area for before and after this time. It's easier when they know what they're looking for."

"Has Owen seen these images? If this is the guy he saw at Negrescu's trailer and he's in some way connected with Jimmy Boy here, then there's a chance he knows Stella and that he wasn't just having a piss or being nosy. He is in some way connected with our latest corpse."

Chapter Twenty Two

The call came through to say that Julie was waiting downstairs. Cyril's heart fluttered a little as his mind rewound the hours. She was sitting in the Reception area flipping through a rather dog-eared magazine. On seeing Cyril approach she tossed it back onto the table.

"Come and sit outside, it's warm in the sun," she said with a broad smile. "You said they come in threes. Always be careful what you wish for Cyril." She let her hand touch his arm.

She was correct about both observations; the sun was warming as they sat on a bench that was shaded from the breeze.

"Another body found after what looks like an organised dog attack in the Brunswick Tunnel."

"The where?" Julie asked, screwing up her face and tipping her head to one side.

Cyril had forgotten that many newcomers to Harrogate knew little or nothing about the tunnel and that even some long-term residents had seldom or never heard of it. It was a part of Harrogate's hidden past, he explained. He also mentioned the injured police officer and the fact that there were links to Drew Sadler.

"I'm hoping you'll be able to get involved with Dr Samual and share ideas. I'd feel comfortable with you keeping an eye on both autopsies just to maintain continuity."

"He'll only be dealing in what he finds, the cold facts. There's likely to be a second autopsy considering the circumstances of death, just as in Drew Sadler's case. Cyril, the cold evidence doesn't change with whoever does the investigating and as SIO in both cases, you'll be along for the ride all the way, but if it keeps you smiling, I'll have a word."

***

It might have been the clinical appearance and the stainless steel, the lighting or the unusual indescribable aroma; it was strangely an aroma that seemed to disappear after a short time of being there. Cyril loathed this element of his work and hoped in his heart of hearts that he never would get used to it.

He looked down onto the mangled remains and his mind flashed back to the young, angry man who had arrogantly leaned back on his chair at their first meeting. He found it hard to comprehend that this was the same face that had stared so disrespectfully. Cyril followed the snake tattoo down from his neck until it arrived at the edge of a piece of flesh that had been opened up to form a large, jagged hole. The snake disappeared. It re-emerged further down at the opposite edge. It then turned round the man's back before appearing to rise up the left side. The edges of the puncture wounds that seemed to pepper his white, almost translucent skin took on a strange, waxy appearance, as if they were almost false. The pubic bone was exposed and only part of the scrotum remained, hanging like a piece of limp, wrinkled stocking.

"The heart is a strong muscle, Chief Inspector, but the human body knows when enough is enough. Massive blood loss, severe damage to the limbs, particularly the extremities, fingers missing, genitals, parts of each ear as you've seen. Large chunks of flesh have been removed from the torso and lower and upper limbs. We should be able to confirm a dog breed from the bite."

The Doctor moved to the bottom of the table.

"Interestingly, the man was first attacked from behind, the calf muscle has been torn away here."

The Doctor pointed out some hanging muscle behind the leg.

"Most of the wounds are on the front and sides of the torso suggesting he was predominantly in a foetal position or on his back during the attack. Another interesting observation is the big toe. It has been partially severed by what appears to be a sharp object, probably glass, whilst he was running. We've taken glass from the scene and we'll investigate that further so obviously a pre-death injury. There's evidence too to suggest that he had fallen from some height, definitely pre-attack, that is, apart from the two injuries I've just described. X-rays show there to be a fracture to the left clavicle and shoulder dislocation. It appears he'd climbed the wall and then tumbled backwards before falling on this portion of the body."

He pointed to the left side.

"There were also blood spatter and runs on the front of the wall which clearly shows heavy bleeding from a leg wound. The majority of body fluids were found behind the wall where the major attack occurred. You might like to see how this head torch has remained almost intact and in place."

The Doctor moved sideways to allow Cyril to take a closer inspection.

Cyril looked up, his mouth slightly ajar. "It's attached with staples!"

"It's obvious that it wasn't meant to be removed. Strange game some people play with their fellow human beings."

"Thank you very much. Toxicology result, Dr Samual?"

"The impossible we do now…" he didn't need to finish.

Cyril smiled and shook his hand. "Did Dr Pritchett have a word?"

"There's always one hundred per cent co-operation between us as you well know. We endeavour to consult and therefore miss nothing."

***

Owen looked at the remnants of the burned-out van. The ground around had been turned to mud in putting out the flames. Considering the Fire Fighters had a six-mile dash, they had managed, at least, to save a small part of the van that was furthest from the diesel tank from being totally consumed in the blaze. He approached one of the team who had just finished photographing and collecting objects for further examination and investigation.

"Nothing human or animal left in there, I take it?" He smiled, resigning himself to a look of disdain and a firm denial.

"Two dogs in a cage in the back. Pity the owner wasn't in a bloody cage in the front!" answered the young woman dressed in white, a mask dangling round her neck. She carried a camera, responded and gave Owen a look that could curdle milk.

Owen took a step back. '*Bloody hell*', he thought, '*she bites!*'

She approached him, holding the camera so that he could see the large screen on the back.

"Large dogs too, evidence of being muzzled here, see? And here. Can you see? Even you should be able to just about make it out." She flicked on. "Captive bolt gun and here we have what appears to be the remains of a stun baton." She looked again closely. "See the part there to the front? There's not much left but I'm pretty sure. I'll know more when I can take an in-depth peek. All three items suggest dog fighting. Here's their dog's medical kit."

Owen tilted his head slightly whilst looking at the image on screen. "What is it?"

"It's what's left of a staple gun. Here look. I know there's not much left and the plastic parts have melted, but that's what it is. Used to stitch the cuts on the dog's flesh. You're dealing with hard, evil bastards here, Sergeant."

"Say not a word as I shouldn't be telling you this, but you might feel a bit better about the dogs if you knew that they were probably used to attack and kill a human being last night and that he might not have been the first. Also attacked a colleague who was attending the scene. You must keep that to yourself but your team will be informed officially very soon once the pathologist's report is released. So, as usual, we need everything you can find. Everything!"

Owen could see the change of expression on the girl's face. "You're joking!"

She could see from Owen's expression that he was not. "We'll fine tooth comb it when we get it back, trust me."

"Simple question, forgive me, but I'm a simple copper. Deliberate? Arson?"

"Without doubt."

Owen made his way to the car to ring in.

"Owen, Sir. It's our burned out van, remains of two dogs, captive bolt gun and other evidence. They'll go through it more thoroughly when it's back at the lab."

"See Liz when you get back in. She has something to show you but don't get too excited!"

***

Sanda was in the kitchen at *Zingaro*. Hai Yau watched her preparing the food from the far side of the room and he was enthralled by her natural flair.

"Sanda, your preparation, your light hand with pastry and your eye for presentation are the best we have in this kitchen and in many of the kitchens I've worked in. You have cooked before I can tell!"

"At home, in Romania, my mother and grandmother were wonderful cooks considering the ingredients they worked with. We grew much and my mother improvised. We had wonderful soups of course, sausages and stuffed peppers. She made everything, even yoghurts and cheeses. It was wonderful fun. Nothing went to waste in our home."

Sanda paused and Hai Yau could see that she was thinking of happier times.

"She taught me and I'll teach my daughter our traditional cuisine one day."

"You could be my top chef, Sanda. That would mean that you'd then have your own room here and more money to send home. Let's see in a few weeks how things progress. We could even make some traditional, Romanian dishes to put on our daily menus."

He came over, put his hands on her shoulders. She stiffened. '*Surely, not the old man too?*' she thought.

He simply kissed her, as a father would a daughter, on each cheek. We'll work together and I'll watch. You have a future and I believe you'll go far in this family. Now, we have a full house tonight and tomorrow, we must continue to prepare."

Sanda relaxed, annoyed that she had totally misread the situation. Her mind reflected on what he had said. This is what she had moved to England for, to be appreciated, to be valued, for a better life. She smiled at Hai Yau. Suddenly she felt unthreatened by the man who controlled her life.

"Thank you. I'll do what I can to repay your faith in me."

***

Cezar removed one dog from its cage before walking it around the back of the barn, his grip firmly on the collar. The dog squirmed and bounced eager to be released; it was choking with the twisting and tightening of its collar. He had, in his other hand, a large knife. The grass in this area was high, mixed with weeds and nettles marking an area that had once been covered with stone outbuildings. Now, only small, derelict stone walls were in evidence. Behind this, a large concrete, rectangular lid had been slipped sideways. Cezar could not appreciate the aroma of freshly cut grass that lingered from the crushing movement of the slab lid. His sense of smell was invaded by the stench that rose from the dark mouth of the pit. He peered into the gaping hole.

It always amazed him the way that the dogs sensed different situations; they knew when there was food, when they were to fight and when there was a chance of sex, but they also sensed danger. The muzzled dog tried to move away, twisting and writhing in a desperate attempt to escape his grip. Cezar's hand twisted the collar more tightly as the dog backed away from the hole that was directly ahead. Its paws pushed forward, trying to find purchase on the dewy grass. Its survival instincts heightened. Without fuss, Cezar expertly changed the position of his body, placing the dog between his knees to hold it still. Gently he positioned the blade between the dog's upper ribs and smiled. With one swift movement he pushed and then twisted. The dog gave a high-pitched yelp, its body bucked away from the blade and then its life ended. Nerves carried on protesting as the twitching carcass was kicked forward. It dropped into the dark before making a splash into what sounded like thick, oozing mud. Moving the blade gently through the top layer of dirt

Cezar cleaned it; he had done this many times in war zones but never after killing dogs. You had to keep the blade clean and sharp. He had always been given the task of dispatching the captured enemy because they knew how much he enjoyed it. He returned for the second dog and began to whistle as the sun hit his face.

Angel had finished with the girl and she was back in the barn cleaning when Cezar returned for the last dog. He held the knife up and grinned. She noticed, as usual, the missing teeth and backed away keeping the brush she held in front of her. He had, however, little interest in a woman this morning. He had much to do and his pleasure now was in despatching the next dog.

***

For their first Saturday, the restaurant was fully booked. Angel was thrilled by the reception they had received and the local advertising had paid off. He had never seen his father look so happy. His mother too sat looking proudly at their latest venture. It was what they had planned and worked so hard for. In three weeks, his father would return home for a while and by that time the kitchen should be in a position to function without him.

***

Joan finished packing her small, overnight bag. She couldn't remember the last time she had felt so excited. It was that mixed tingle of fear and uncertainty that took her back to the heady frisson she had experienced before those teenage dates. She checked herself, as it all seemed so utterly ridiculous. She kissed the children and her father. Mrs Baines stood, a dichotomy with her dominant stance wrapped in a floral apron tied around her waist, fluffy slippers on her feet. There was little to no affection in her eyes.

"Are you sure you're doing the right thing? You hardly know the person."

It was as if Mrs Baines couldn't bring herself to say the word, man!

"I'll be back late Sunday afternoon, mother. Remember, I'm a big girl. I'll ring when I'm shopping. Is there anything you'd like me to get?"

"Just get back here safely and don't do anything you'll regret."

Joan was half expecting a lecture on the sins of the flesh but she was spared that. The knock at the door had something to do with it. Joan went to answer.

"Come in and meet the family, you know the kids."

Peter Anton ran his hand through his hair and took a deep breath.

"She'll not bite you, well I hope not!" whispered Joan whilst pulling a face that showed ambivalence.

"Great! Into the valley of death..." he muttered under his breath in response.

Mr and Mrs Baines stood in the parlour. Joan immediately noticed that her mother had removed the apron and didn't look quite so stern. Maybe she was more anxious than she made out.

"This is Peter."

Mr Baines moved across and held out his hand. "Reg, Peter. Nice to meet you, may I introduce my wife and Joan's mother..."

"Mrs Baines," she interrupted setting out a line, not in sand on this occasion, but in the pattern of the Axminster.

Joan scowled at her mother before collecting her bag.

"Looks like we're going. It was a pleasure to meet you both," said Peter as he was thankfully ushered out into the hall. He felt like an unwanted salesman.

Nothing else was said until they were in the car.

"I don't like him Reg, he has a weak chin, his shoes lacked polish and I'm sure I've seen him before."

Reg just looked at his wife and shook his head. "Give the girl a bloody chance and stop being so bloody evil, mother!"

Barbara Baines turned to look at Reg. She couldn't remember the last time she had heard him raise his voice at her and she had certainly never heard him swear! It brought a flutter of excitement to her tummy and she had to sit down.

Chapter Twenty Three

Joan opened the door with the plastic credit card key. The room was perfect if not a little bizarre. Large black and white tiles chequered the expanse of floor leading to the folding balcony doors. Red leather furniture contrasted with the floor only to be complemented by large modern splash paintings boldly decorating the walls. It should not have been pleasing to the eye but somehow it worked. It was a serviced apartment situated a short walk from the main shopping area.

"I've booked this because it offers everything a hotel should and much more. I hope you like it? I thought it daring!"

From the look on Joan's face he could see that she loved it. She stepped out onto the long balcony and breathed deeply.

"It's perfect. What time's your meeting?"

"It's half an hour away so I'm leaving after a coffee." He moved and stood behind her kissing her neck. "Sorry I don't have time but…"

"You'll be late and I'll miss some vital shopping time."

Peter handed her an envelope. "Open it when I've gone and enjoy it. You may spend what I earn today. It's your good girl present for managing to get your…" He paused putting his finger to his lips as if deep in thought. "Mother, I think the word is I should be looking for, to agree to this."

"You shouldn't."

Peter smiled, happy that she had not protested too much.

He picked up his small brief case and left.

Once alone, she opened the envelope. There was £500 in crisp, new notes. She smiled to herself.

Within twenty minutes Peter's car passed the two dogs of Foo that stood guarding the Chinese gate to the Cash and Carry. He parked by the door and climbed out. The aroma of smoked bacon drifted from the transport café opposite, swamping his sense of smell and reminding him that he had not eaten. He was too nervous. The door was answered, opened with an electronic click and he pushed it ajar. He knew both of the people facing him. They bowed slightly before shaking his hand.

"It's good to see you Peter, come and sit."

Considering the circumstances under which they met, Peter was always touched by the hospitality and welcome he received, but then, as in all business life, holding on to a degree of scepticism was never a disadvantage. It was a wonderful feeling to sit with these people, respected, liked and no longer in their debt. To have weathered that storm and come through safely had not been easy. The one key factor in his mind for this transition had been leaving Stella, but then a firm understanding of the dire, physical consequences that the downward spiral of gambling had brought inculcated in him a sharp lesson and a return to his senses. He felt as though he were now respected.

Peter removed the package from the brief case and placed it on the table.

"It's come full circle," he smiled. "But with it there's a bonus."

He passed a second package.

"We've taken only our handling fee. Sadly, that avenue of work has been closed but others are waiting on the side-line. However, first we must wait to see if there are repercussions. Our Scottish friends may yet prove troublesome."

The two men looked at the packages and then back at Peter.

"All is as it should be, you can trust me!" he emphasised.

**

A steaming latte sat in front of Joan, a brown heart formed in the white froth of milk. She had smiled at the barista who had looked her up and down as he handed her the drink. The coffee gave her the impetus to ring home.

"It's me, how are you? And how are the kids? Behaving themselves I hope."

She listened and smiled as her father complimented her on their upbringing. She put her finger in the froth of the coffee going for the centre of the heart and then licked it.

"Love you too, Dad."

She waited, as instructed for her mother to come to the phone.

"What have I done or is it the kids?"

Joan listened and the smile fell from her lips.

"Are you sure? You're not just making this up to spoil the one good thing I have going in my miserable life are you? Why can't you be more like dad?"

She immediately regretted the last sentence and apologised.

The coffee was cold by the time she had eventually brought her mental confusion under some control. She decided that it would be easier to simply confront him. She checked her watch. He would be back in under the hour.

***

The Royal Victoria Hospital was experiencing the usual busy Saturday in the Accident and Emergency Department but in the High Dependency Unit all was calm apart from the plethora of electronic sounds playing discordantly, constantly signalling that things were either as they should be or were going catastrophically wrong. The dedicated nurses seemed to blank out the former whilst listening constantly for the latter, in some patients' cases with a degree more expectation.

At 14:26 the alarm sounded as Jim's vital body functions started to close down, the specialist had been correct in his initial, pessimistic diagnosis. There was no panic, just an intensity of movement and attention as different personnel focussed on the small man who was being kept alive by cables, tubes and wires. At 15:00 he was no longer a concern. His monitors were blank and the space he had occupied for the last few days was now empty.

***

Joan was nursing a large glass of red wine when Peter returned. He smiled and moved towards her before kissing her forehead. He checked his watch and looked at the glass but decided to say nothing. He noticed the bags stacked carefully by the bed and smiled.

"It looks as though you had a successful day."

He poured himself a wine, walked over and touched her glass. She remained silent.

"Have I done something? Not done something?"

Joan turned looking directly at him. She had a great deal of practice in dealing with the vagaries of the human male in all its underhand, cheating and malevolent forms.

"When you gave me the invitation for the restaurant and told me to invite mum, you said you couldn't go, you were, in your very words, '*Busy that evening*'.

Peter frowned. "That's true. I was, believe me, I was."

"You know we left early that night and it was embarrassing because my mother didn't give a reason, she just said it was important that we leave. So, to keep the peace, we did."

Peter said nothing but his expression demanded an explanation.

"I thought today was the first time that you'd met but she's told me that she's seen you before; she couldn't recall at first where but then it came to her. Now where might she have seen you, Peter Anton?"

Peter smiled and moved his hand on hers.

"She obviously saw me at the restaurant if she had cause to leave. I was there about nine. Am I correct? I've never set eyes on her in my life, I still don't recall seeing her there. So how come I upset her?"

"I don't know. She just said that she saw you there, nothing else. Probably the fact that I'd told her that you couldn't get there and then surprise, surprise! She now knows that you were there. I don't know what's going on so why were you there?"

"Did you pay for your meal when you left?"

"No, it was free, on the house, it was an invitation to the restaurant to try the food."

"That's correct. Did you pay for your drinks apart from the complimentary Champagne?"

"No, the owner's son said that it had been taken care of and so we left."

"I was there to leave money behind the bar to 'take care' of your drinks' bill. I wanted the evening to be on me. I simply popped in, paid some money and went straight out."

He could see Joan beginning to blush. She put her head down and he noticed her shoulders lift as if she were sobbing. He leaned over and wrapped a protective arm around her.

"Had I recognised your mother today, from seeing her that night, I would have said, but I didn't see her."

"I'm sorry, Peter. Will I ever be able to trust a man again?"

"'Course you will. It'll take time, but that's all it takes to heal the invisible wounds, time. And Joan, the one thing we do have is time."

***

Cezar had tidied up. The concrete cover was back over the old septic tank and he was now preparing to collect the necessary takings from Hai Yau's various business interests and ensure that the staff was behaving. He enjoyed this part of the work, particularly visiting the working girls. Strangely, he never saw himself as their pimp just their intimate friend. They saw him as neither, just a necessary evil to get out of their lives as quickly and as painlessly as possible. It would take him until the early hours.

Follifoot was quiet, it always was and at five on a Sunday it would have been like the grave apart from the enthusiastic chorus of singing birds trying to drag in the new day. Cezar had parked the van with other vehicles on the narrow main street, opposite The Harewood Arms pub. It would take him only a few minutes to reach his destination. He walked up the empty drive and made his way along the side of the house. He did not need a torch. Getting in the house was easy; he simply pulled a key from his pocket, found the lock, turned the key and entered. The warning beep of the alarm made him move swiftly to the box on the wall and enter the numbers. The sound stopped. For some reason, that process always made him panic a little. He went to the kettle, shook it gently and switched it on. He had a long wait there that day but he had been out most of the night. He would have a coffee, some breakfast and then sleep.

It was late in the afternoon when Cezar heard the car pull onto the drive. He remained seated facing the door. He heard the key in the lock and the door open.

"I might have bloody guessed," said Peter, realising he had a guest. The alarm's warning call had not registered his entry.

"Surely you knew and are thrilled to see me! How was she?"

Cezar put his tongue out and waggled it salaciously.

Peter walked into the lounge. It was like a tip, two plates had been left out, the paper was spread on the floor, two beer bottles and a wine bottle were still where they had been dropped.

"Why the hell don't you clear up?"

"Woman's work, fucking woman's work, that's why!"

"I suppose the bedroom is the same."

"Same shit, just a different room."

In front of Cezar on the cluttered coffee table were three piles of cash comprising bundles of notes bound with elastic bands. Peter walked over and picked them up.

"Another good week. Angel will be thrilled, what with the restaurant's success, Rares out of the way and now to finish the week, this!"

He held a bundle pressing the end of the notes against his thumb, allowing them to run through whilst trapped by the elastic band, as if they were a deck of cards.

Cezar grinned. "It's all from my good girls, welfare and other benefits payments, rents, it all adds up. The news of Rares has already spread to Leeds. I got the distinct impression that these employees don't fucking like me. Strange that." He grinned whilst removing some dirt from under a fingernail with his knife.

Peter opened the brief case and tossed the package across the table; it was half of the money received from James Nolan.

"I take it this will not be going back to the family?"

"What they don't know won't hurt them, besides they've got enough and I do more than enough. The time I wasn't in the tunnel they killed the wrong bloody guy and who was it who cleaned up after them?"

"This time you screwed it up completely, it was a shambles," said Peter. "Fun to watch though."

"Don't be too sure, my friend, that it was a cock-up. God moves in mysterious ways."

"If Angel finds out that you are dealing behind his back, what then?"

"It's been going on fucking ages. He'll not be strong forever, believe me."

Peter could see by his eyes that his words were sincere.

"Did you know that your girl's mother nearly shit herself when she spotted me at the restaurant talking to you? Fucking battle-axe. Never thought she'd pay up Sadler's debt. Probably could have taken her for more. Yes, she did a runner straight after seeing me, never had her pudding. If she goes to the fucking coppers I'll have her grandkids whether I swing for it or not."

Cezar looked at Peter's face. "Don't you come on all innocent with me, you sold the stuff or let's say you tempted him to buy."

Peter just looked at him. "Say all that again and say it slowly." He listened. A penny fell somewhere in his head. "Oh shit!"

Chapter Twenty-Four

Cyril drank an espresso whilst staring at the Theodore Major painting. Each time he looked at it, he found another element in the detail, either in the colour used or in the way the paint had been applied. Somehow it looked different at varying times of the day, maybe the changes in his daily moods had something to do with the way he interpreted what he observed. The sound of the duo *Fingersnap* singing 'Blackbirds' on the iPod seemed to fill the room with warmth. Cyril closed his eyes as he inhaled the menthol vapour from his e cigarette and smiled. His mind turned to Julie and he wondered whether she would like to try the Zingaro Restaurant again later in the week. He washed and dried the cup and saucer before putting it away. He checked the room, as always, it was immaculate.

Once at his office, Cyril's start to the day was a ritual. Coat on a hanger and then on to the coat-stand by the door, jacket draped behind the chair. He would then glance at the files and assess any notes marked for his urgent attention in order to prioritise his schedule. Finally, it came to the necessary evil, the computer. The first note he saw informed him of James Nolan death. He wrote a memo to contact the officer in charge to determine whether Jim had regained consciousness before he died. He needed to find out if they had discovered more footage of the victim or the vehicle.

Owen tapped on the door.

"Morning, Sir. Trust your weekend went well?"

"Great, thanks and yours?" He didn't give him time to answer. "Did Liz ask you to check the CCTV of the man with Jim Nolan at the bus station? He's died by the way. Was it the chap you saw at Negrescu's trailer?"

Owen stood back as if bowled over by the flood of questions, miming that he was holding a cricket bat and driving away Cyril's requests for information. Cyril frowned.

"Weekend was great, yes, I have, yes." He swung round as if driving an imaginary ball for six. "I think it is, yes." He put both hands in the air. "Three boundaries, all before nine and a coffee; comes of being a Yorkshire lad."

Owen could see that Cyril was losing patience so he pretended to stand his imaginary bat against Cyril's desk.

"The technical lads are trying to improve the images but they can't get rid of the man's bloody cap no matter what they do!"

Owen smiled cautiously but realised that Cyril had taken him seriously believing that the latest technology could do the impossible like extract facial features that were hidden from view. He did not enlighten him as it appeared that his boss had climbed out of the wrong side of the bed that morning, so he gave him some information that Cyril was not expecting.

"I've had a look at the footage taken from the taxi's in-car camera again, too. In fact, I sat and watched the whole sixty-four gigs worth on Sunday. Firstly, I'm sure our driver is the same guy I saw at the trailer, remember, Sir, the one with the skeleton bandana. If you compare his height with the size of the truck, it's about right. Earlier in the evening the footage shows that Ms Hutler overtakes a similar truck near the Grammar School on Arthurs Avenue. On close inspection I can't see or make out a registration plate. I've added the make and model of what I think to be the vehicle to the ANPR National Data Centre and there aren't as many vehicles matching that description in the North East as you might think. I have a list of owners and registration numbers but as the one we saw on Pannal Road didn't show a number, it's going to take some poor Investigating Officer quite a while to track down, but you just never know."

"Good work. Where's Liz?"

Owen just shrugged his shoulders. "There was a call from Mr Baines. Wanted to speak with me A.S.A.P. about something his wife has said. He wants to call here, on his own. Maybe she's told him she that loves him and now he believes she's putting powdered glass in his tea." Owen grinned.

"Good theory, my learned friend, but there's one thing wrong with that."

"What?"

"She doesn't make the tea, he does!"

Owen pulled a face. "He's coming in at ten."

***

Sanda was the first in the kitchen. Every Monday the restaurant was closed and so there would be a full clean and some preparation of staff meals. Hai Yau would not be in until later. Angel was there early in what was known as the office, but in reality it was where he sat for most of the time drinking coffee, following up orders and holding meetings with different associates. She noticed him watching her and she felt uneasy. Her mind went back to the barn and then to Rares and she contemplated what might have happened to him, she had not seen him for a while. The last time she had seen him was at the farm as she left. She remembered the conversation between Angel and his father, she recalled the word dogs and the word Darkie; that was enough, she felt the pangs of unease again. She looked across at the block containing various kitchen knives and vowed she would use one if he came over and tried to fondle her again.

Various vehicles arrived in the car park that morning, usually making deliveries. Staff went out to collect them before they were itemised, audited and the dates checked before storing. A system was beginning to develop and there was a more relaxed atmosphere in the kitchen. More and more of the staff looked to Sanda for guidance, as she seemed to be in favour with Hai Yau.

A green van pulled into the car park. Cezar and Karl climbed out. Sanda stared from the kitchen and could see the anxiety etched on the boy's face. It made her nervous. She had seen the same look in Rares' eyes when she had seen him in the barn.

When Karl came into the kitchen, Sanda went to him. She smiled, her face full of concern.

"Where's Rares? Have you seen him?"

The youth turned to her and burst into tears.

***

Mr Baines refused tea. "I'm sorry to take your time, Sergeant, but I feel I had to come and say something, even though she said it would be of no use. It was something my wife said. We had a bit of …let us say, a to-do on Saturday. Let me try to explain. Last week my wife and daughter were invited to the opening of the new restaurant on Otley Road, you know the one, the Italian place that used to be *The Beehive*? Well your Inspector was there. Mrs Baines went to the toilet during the meal and saw a man in the passageway talking, the very same man who had come to our home demanding money that was owed to him by Drew. It was three thousand pounds he was demanding. We were both shocked, as you can imagine. He told us that nothing would happen to us if it were not paid but then he assured us that he would make Drew pay by harming the children. He also said that if we were to report his visit to the police, then irrespective of payment, the children would be the first to suffer."

"You failed to mention this when we called. When was this?"

"The threats, Sergeant, the threats. Why would we mention it? It was months ago, I have the date when I withdrew the cash."

"How sure was Mrs Baines that it was the same man?"

"Once you've seen him, you'd not really forget him. When she came home she was in a state. Joan thought her mother had drunk too much, or something didn't suit, thought she was just spoiling things again, as usual, but I know that she was truly frightened."

***

Cyril spoke with the officer in charge of the incident involving Jim Nolan.

"Never regained consciousness. No clues around where he was found but we're now sure that a bag was taken. Witnesses from the bus suggest he was carrying the bag seen on the incident footage but none was found at the scene. We do see it being removed by the suspect. Nothing has been found dumped locally. We have some CCTV of people waiting at the bus station. I've taken footage from an hour before the arrival of the Edinburgh National Express coach and that's available now for you. It's simply a case of working backwards but I can't see someone waiting much longer than that."

Cyril sat upright when he was told how he should do his job but thanked the officer.

He brought the footage up on screen and two officers who were in the incident room walked across at his request. It was strange watching the bus pull out in reverse, people walking backwards, but then Cyril's finger hit the keypad to pause the image. There he was, same coat and same cap. He was sitting sideways with a view of the National Express stop.

"Bingo! It's our man from Harrogate Bus Station. He seems to give out with one hand and take back with the other. Looks like drugs. All we have to do now is find out who this bastard is."

***

As soon as Mr Baines mentioned the man being taller than Owen, he could have pencilled in the rest of the description but he resisted leading the witness. It all came out, one piece after the other.

"Notice anything else?"

Reg thought. "Yes, he had a strange accent, probably foreign but saying that, he had a flat, Yorkshire accent but you could still tell he was from abroad."

"So what did you do?"

"We paid, of course, what else do you do when confronted by someone who seemed as callous as anyone I've ever known? He was evil in fact."

"I don't suppose he told you why your son-in-law owed the money?"

"Drugs I assume as he said that the money had gone up his nose. We couldn't pay him then and there, of course, we don't keep a lot of money in the house, even though we don't need a guard dog with Barbara there all the time. We told him that we'd need to draw on some savings. He gave us three days!"

"Reasonable of him! And? I take it Barbara is Mrs Baines?"

"Yes, you recognised the description, sorry. He didn't come back in three days, he came back five days later, early in the morning and took the money."

"How sure were you that he wouldn't keep returning until he'd cleared your accounts?"

"Mrs Baines. She threatened that if he were to either touch the children or return she would personally see that he would hang!"

He sat back and folded his arms and smiled as if in admiration of his wife.

"Those were her exact words."

"Right, I see. So why tell us now."

"Goodness, I'm forgetting myself and the main reason I came. It was the connection, you see."

"Connection, Mr Baines?"

"When she saw him in the restaurant, she saw him talking to another chap. She hadn't met him until Saturday when the very same chap called at our home. She didn't put two and two together at first. She knew she'd seen him before but she just couldn't remember where and then it came to her."

"So who is he?"

"Peter Anton, my daughter's new boyfriend, the man she spent the weekend with, the man who was a friend of Drew."

Owen just looked up. "Your daughter doesn't know you're here does she?"

Reg shook his head.

"Does your daughter know about this money and the threats?"

"She only knows that Barbara recognised her boyfriend at the restaurant, that she'd told Barbara that he was supposed to be busy that night, that's why he gave the ticket for them to attend. I can assure you, Sergeant, that Barbara doesn't like her daughter's new man, call it a woman's intuition, I don't know and I think she'd do anything to get Joan to see through him."

"Even lie, Mr Baines? Would Barbara make up stories to frighten Joan off every man she meets? Does Barbara's very existence not rely on having a large degree of control over the grandchildren's future and Joan's and, if you don't mind my saying so, yours?"

"I'm sorry, I've obviously wasted your time and mine. I neither came here to be insulted, Sergeant, nor did I come to justify my wife's strange way of caring, but I did come for help. I can now see that you think the whole thing is a sham, a work of fiction on my wife's part. I'll bid you good day."

Reg stood, moved to the door, paused and turned to face Owen.

"Should anything happen, Sergeant Owen, to any of my family, I'll hold you personally responsible. What I've told you has been written down and signed by both myself and Barbara and is in the safe keeping of my solicitor with strict instructions as to when it should be opened."

**

The incident room was full. The evidence, like pieces of a jigsaw puzzle, was slowly coming together.

"It all seems to fall on this one man. Spotted at the side of the road at the time Drew Sadler's body was dumped, at the death of Negrescu and the attack on the police officer. Involved and possibly responsible for the attack and subsequent murder of James Nolan, DNA for two rapes over a number of years and possibly more, probably involved in dog fighting and God only knows what else. We have a perfect description from one of our own, Owen here, and we hold his DNA. But he's a ghost. Despite his height and features, nobody's seen him."

"Joan's mother has, Sir, and as to being a ghost, he was also right under your nose whilst you dined out at the opening night of Zingaro last week."

The room fell silent. Owen explained the meeting with Mr Baines in detail.

"We've pussy-footed around Peter Bloody Anton twice and now we find he knows this man. I want him arrested and I want him in this afternoon. I also want you and Liz to go and talk with Mr and Mrs Baines. I want a twenty-four hour watch on the house. If threats have been made, considering this man's track record, I don't want a Harrogate citizen's abduction and murder on my record. Find out where the kids attend school and have a word with the Head Teacher, her staff need to be vigilant but I want confidentiality."

"We can do a search of Anton's property for drugs and DNA without a warrant. Might be a long shot but our man might have been there if they know each other," Owen offered.

"No problem." Cyril reassured on procedurals. "There's a fear of child abduction and that'll be upheld. Inform him when you make the arrest. Get the Forensic team in and make the search thorough. Anything on the vehicles, the one seen on the night Drew Sadler was dumped?"

"Still working through the list, Sir. We're visiting addresses rather than phoning for details; the likelihood is that if they feel we're close, the vehicle will be destroyed. We've two addresses where owners had similar flat-bed trucks but the vehicles have been scrapped recently."

"Prioritise those."

Cyril tapped his electronic cigarette against his chin as if to aid his thought process.

"I'll pop along and pay Angel and his father a visit. Stuart, you may be my chaperone. I want information back in here by this afternoon, 15:00 briefing and I want Peter Anton sweating in interview room four before then, even if it means dragging him from work."

Cyril passed his desk and glanced down at a note.

'Drew Sadler's body will be released tomorrow. Funeral has been arranged for Thursday 2pm. Second autopsy concluded, no surprises! Everyone has pulled out the stops to get the cremation as quickly as possible for the sake of the bereaved. Julie.'

Frustrated, he checked his diary, remembering Liz's promise, it was the last thing he wanted to add to his busy week at this stage of the investigation.

**

Angel welcomed Cyril with a firm handshake and a smile. Cyril introduced DC Park. They moved through to the office.

"Coffee, gentleman?"

Both declined.

"Do you have a surname?" Cyril asked unsure as to whether he had mentioned it when they were first introduced.

"Yau, my father's."

"Your real father, Mr Yau?" Cyril responded whilst maintaining firm eye contact.

"No, I was adopted at a young age and I don't know my original surname only my Christian name. Yes, Inspector, don't look too surprised, I'm a Christian. My real name is Wadim but the name Angel was given to me for some reason when I was very young, I don't know or care why," he lied. "What's this about? You're certainly not here to ask about my family history."

Cyril noted that he not only looked him in the eye but that he also seemed relaxed.

"What is your connection with Peter Anton, Mr Yau?"

"He's my father's accountant, has been for a couple of years. Chinese business friends recommended him to us and so far, his work has been excellent. You're sitting in the proof of that financial guidance. We're one of Mr Anton's private clients. As you know most accountants have them."

"And what about this gentleman?"

Cyril passed him an EvoFIT image of the man Owen had seen at Rares Negrescu's trailer.

Angel looked at it. Shook his head and handed it back.

"No, sorry! With a face like that you think he'd be easily recognised. We've many people using our restaurant. Delivery drivers come and go, workers, health inspectors, even Police Inspectors!"

Cyril looked at Stuart. He was unhappy with the flippant answer.

"Go and bring all the staff and line them up outside that door. I'll show them the photo one at a time and if they all concur with you, Mr Yau, then we're wasting your time and more importantly, ours."

"I'm sorry but they're busy. Is it normal to just come uninvited into someone's business and make unreasonable demands? Do you not require some kind of warrant?"

"Did you see that rat, Stuart? Goodness it was a big one! There's another!" Cyril pointed behind Angel.

Stuart had never taken his eyes off Angel.

"Saw both, sir. Want me to ring Environmental Health? They'd probably only close the place for a few days if they're lucky. It'd make the time for your staff to take a look at this picture and answer a few questions with our translators. Wouldn't you agree, Mr Yau?"

"You can't do that!" he protested, but then paused considering his options. "Bring them!"

Stuart went out and into the kitchen. The staff proved to be like a flock of sheep. '*If you kicked one they would all limp*', Cyril thought. He certainly could have kicked himself for not organising a translator as unfortunately he had to rely on Angel translating, and from looking at his body language, he had escaped lightly. To be honest, Cyril had expected Angel to simply recognise the man then there would not have been the need for all this. He had thought that he would have had a simple and innocent justification for his being there, not having to resort to hiding behind lies.

It was very obvious that the staff looked constantly for guidance from Angel who glared at each and spoke rapidly. Although there was consistency in the question he asked, Cyril detected that some points made were specific and judging by the facial expressions of some of the staff, threatening. Cyril could prove nothing. Not surprisingly, no one recognised the photo-fit image. Angel smiled and thanked each as they left and Cyril could almost feel their relief.

It wasn't until he saw Sanda enter did he sit up. As with the others, he wrote down her name. He remembered witnessing her sadness on the opening night and would have given anything to speak with her alone. He would organise that, but it would not be now. He also noted that she was not as cowed as the others, she neither looked at Angel nor, from her attitude, feared him. She spent longer looking at the photograph too. She turned to Angel and spoke quickly.

"She says that my father knows him, he's a Romany and he called to collect some scrap materials that were stored at the back of the restaurant. She remembers that my father was annoyed because he was late, it should have been cleared in the afternoon. My father gave him food in the kitchen, which is why he was inside. I personally knew nothing of this arrangement."

Cyril stood, aware of the surprise on Angel's face. It was true that this was the first time he had heard the story. Maybe he had been telling the truth all along. Cynically, Cyril still held a small percentage of doubt.

"Thank you very much. I'd like a copy of all your employees' details by two this afternoon. And, Mr Yau, I do mean everything."

He checked his watch.

"If all of their paperwork is above board, legal and properly in order, it should be easy for you or your secretary to organise. I'll send an officer to collect." Cyril held up the list. "I know this isn't the full extent of your employees."

The atmosphere between them was decidedly cold, and a state of armed truce seemed now to be in place.

"Where's your father, Mr Yau? I'd like to speak with him to confirm that what," Cyril looked at his list of names, "Sanda has said is the truth."

"He'll be here this afternoon between three and four." Angel smiled.

"That's not what I asked. It would take me one phone call to determine his address. Let's try again. Where is your father now?"

"Tanglewood Farm, off Tang Lane. He should be there. I can call him and check to save you a wasted journey, Inspector."

Cyril just shook his head, rejecting the sarcasm.

"No need, I'm sure one of your staff has already informed him that we're here and that he'll be expecting us."

***

Stuart turned down White Wall Lane before veering onto Tang Lane; it had taken twenty-two minutes. The gate to the farm was closed and Hai Yau was sitting in his car behind it. The area's aroma was definitely agricultural! Stuart looked at Cyril as if to refute that the smell had come from him!

***

Angel went into the kitchen and approached Sanda who stood holding an onion in one hand and a large vegetable knife in the other. She put up the hand holding the onion to suggest he come no closer.

"Did my father tell you to say that?"

She shook her head. "He was here, I saw him, guests saw him and he stands out in any crowd so he cannot be swept under the carpet. At least you now have some time."

"I see you have three precious talents, Sanda. Maybe we could go to your room and discover the first all over again. I can thank you properly."

"I have work and you need to tell your father."

"It's done."

Angel looked into Sanda's eyes, where he saw the same look he had seen as a child in the eyes of the man who had abducted him; a cocktail of purpose and coldness.

"Another time, I hope, another time." He smiled, turning to leave, trying not to lose face.

***

On seeing the car pull up, Hai Yau climbed out. "Inspector Bennett, it's a pleasure to see you again. I remember your kind words to me on our opening night. Angel called to say you were on your way. I stopped here as I was coming to the restaurant to check if the preparation and cleaning are going to plan."

"Chief Inspector, It's Detective Chief Inspector," he corrected. "Would your son not do that?"

"Not in my kitchen. No! No! No! Detective Chief Inspector, sorry," he said, waving his finger. "You have a picture to show me?"

Stuart handed him the photograph.

"I don't know him too well, in fact I know little about him. Others have warned me that he can be an aggressive person, moody and quick to anger. He collects scrap, bits of building materials, metal and the like. One of my staff, who has sadly left for some unknown reason, knew him and that's how I contacted this man. His name is Cezar; I was given a mobile number. When he called at the restaurant, he was late and I was cross. He should have come at three and he came just before nine on the day we opened. You cannot trust these Romany types, Inspector, believe me."

"Angel mentioned that he was himself of Romany origin and seemed proud of his heritage."

"That might be true, but that was when he was a baby, before he was adopted. I trust my son and so can you."

Stuart turned away. He had heard bullshit before and what with the smell, they had it here in spade loads.

"You said his name was Cezar. Do you have a surname? Do you have his number?"

Hai Yau took out his mobile, put on some reading glasses and read out the number. "No surname. Don't know whether that's his real name either."

Cyril tapped the numbers into his phone and it rang. Stuart had copied them onto his pad and he moved away to call the station to get phone records for the number.

The call was answered and a mechanical voice informed Cyril that the person was not available at the moment and to leave a message. Cyril hung up.

"Busy scrap man! Has he been to the restaurant before?"

"He came a couple of times when we were building, but that's all."

"Do you always feed him?"

"Yes, it is part of my culture. I also welcome him to use the bathroom or he would simply use the car park."

Cyril paused at the thought. "Thank you. We'll detain you no longer."

***

The incident room was busy; there was a gentle, but industrious hum of voices. Some officers checked the white boards and others computer screens. Cyril tapped his electronic cigarette on the table. People stopped and found a perch.

"We have a name, Cezar. He's likely to be a Romany, a scrap collector and we have a phone number."

Stuart came straight in. "Phone is untraceable. It's been, if you pardon the term, sir, scrapped. It's a throw away."

"Knew it! Right, speaking of scrapped, what of the two flat bed trucks, Owen?"

"One local. Registered to a Raymond Benson, a local farmer. Sold to a scrap dealer who drove it away, the day before Drew Sadler's body was found."

"Where's the farm?"

"Summerbridge. Officer attending as we speak to see if the buyer is our man but Benson's verbal description indicates that he is."

"Liz, what of Mr and Mrs Baines?"

"Although she seemed angry that Mr Baines had been here, she seemed relieved too. She has no problem with having a watch on the house, but she'd prefer us not to talk to Joan about it. She also identified the man in the photograph as the one who came to collect the money and made the threats."

Owen looked at Liz.

"Sir, the funeral's planned for Thursday. Could bringing Joan in for a chat wait? If we find him before then, fine, if not, then nothing's spoiling. Anton's here and we have him for twenty-four hours, possibly longer."

"Yes, you're right, of course, Liz. I'll attend the funeral with you. It's important that we show our support. Anything else, anyone?"

"Sir, just received a call to say the farmer has confirmed a photo match with the purchaser of his vehicle. The buyer's our man."

"Owen, get over to the farm and get as much info as possible. He was obviously not alone if he drove it away. Anything. See if he has details of the other person and other vehicle. Check if the farm has CCTV. I doubt it, but with more and more rural theft, you never know. Right, go over everything again. Liaise with the team at Anton's place and keep everything up to speed. Miss nothing. Liz, Stuart you're with me. We're going to have a chat with Mr Anton but first I need a coffee and a strong one."

Chapter Twenty Five

It has to be said that the interview room was not a pleasant environment in which to sit alone with only your thoughts and your guilt. A degree of uncertainty and anxiety was clearly evident in Anton's body language; anyone brought in and left alone in an interview room would demonstrate a similar profile. His fingers tapped the table and his opposite foot bounced nervously. The longer he waited, the better. The solitary figure reminded Cyril of Negrescu, they both demonstrated a similar posture and attitude to authority that he concluded must be cultural traits.

Cyril, Liz and Stuart walked in and Peter stood but said nothing initially.

"Mr Anton, my name is Detective Chief Inspector Bennett." He emphasised his rank. "You've met DS Graydon when she read you your rights during your arrest."

Cyril looked up and smiled.

"This is DC Park, I believe you met him at your office, yes? You were read your rights, I take it, Mr Anton, when you were arrested?"

"I need to speak with my lawyer and I'd like him present. I'd like to make a call now!" Anton demanded, the sudden steely look in his eyes seeming to back up his demand.

Cyril passed him his mobile phone and folded his arms.

"The call has to be in private. You know that. I have my own phone. I should like it returning so that I may make the call."

The phone was brought and the three officers left.

It took just over an hour for Anton's lawyer to arrive. Cyril spoke with him, disclosing the reason for his client's arrest. His statement was deliberately brief. He was shown into an office and

Peter was brought in. They shook hands and waited for the door to close.

"Drugs, Peter, handling drugs in connection with Drew Sadler. There is a forensic search of your property, taking place right now. We know that, even though that information was not forthcoming. Why now, do you think?"

"It must be Cezar, they're closing in on him. He told me the other day that he was spotted at the restaurant."

"You're right and believe me Mr Yau is very upset. You're going to talk about your past, you've done it before when you were interviewed at your place of work but whatever you do, say nothing that might implicate the others, apart from Cezar, that is. We've prepared this. Read it."

Both men looked at each other and smiled.

They were returned to the interview room. Liz sat to one side, leaving Cyril to face Peter and his solicitor.

"You know why you've been arrested, Mr Anton? Handling and distributing drugs for favour or financial gain."

There was a long pause.

"At the moment a Forensics' team is working through your property."

Peter looked at his solicitor who nodded and smiled encouragingly.

"I had little choice, Chief Inspector. If I'd not done what was asked of me you'd have been investigating another mysterious, grizzly death. You've yet to meet this man, you have no idea what he's like. I've experienced such men, my stepfather was just the same, pure and bloody evil. In my country people lived under the clenched fist of Communism for years and years and men like Cezar thrived under the protective banner of the Securitate. They were nothing but political thugs who controlled every element of society from assassinations to punishment squads. They even checked if women were having abortions and if so, gave them the choice of prostitution or a lengthy prison sentence. These guys were demonic, they were predictably callous. If you wanted a man to confess to the killing of Jesus Christ, just give him to some of those bastards who lurked in the bowels of the Police buildings; if they didn't confess, they disappeared and if they did confess, they still disappeared: that was the predictability of life in those days. After the revolution, these people, these animals, survived even though they were no longer protected by the new regime. They moved here, to this country and more will come, they will form their own groups and slowly they'll be a major criminal fraternity. So why did I do it? To save my bloody skin."

"Tell me about your first meeting with him."

"I was at University and I found myself in debt, a little gambling. I paid my debts by working every hour I could. I worked at the local Chinese Cash and Carry and managed to repay the money I owed. They employed me after qualifying, as you well know. Sergeant Owen has all my employment details. I was recommended to Hai Yau and he became one of my private clients. I then met a girl, Stella Gornall, who was fun and beautiful but in time she became very demanding emotionally and financially. She told me that she was pregnant and that the child was mine. She started dabbling in drugs and she introduced me to the man who was able to supply her needs. That's how Cezar came into my life. I don't know who contacted whom first but he was soon a part of us."

"So what happened to Stella?" Liz asked. "And what happened to the child?"

"I realised that my life was going down the toilet, more bills, more drugs and then the booze. Eventually we couldn't pay the rent, we couldn't pay for the drugs, no, that's inaccurate, I couldn't pay, Stella sat at home and watched T.V. The place became a tip. Then there were the other guys who called, unbeknown to me at first, but it became obvious as the drugs kept appearing. I couldn't leave her until it dawned on me that she was being pimped by Cezar. Anyway, in the end I had to leave but by this time, Cezar had his claws deeply set in my hide. I'd pass on the occasional package and he kept himself to himself, he wouldn't bother me and that was fine. Without Stella, I started to get my life back under control. Missed Rose though, I guess I still do."

"Who's Rose?" quizzed Liz.

"Our daughter. Stella and me."

Cyril looked at Liz warning her to say nothing.

"Still gambling, Mr Anton?"

"I'm working on curbing my habit. Not like before, but I enjoy playing poker and that's the reason I got involved with Drew Sadler. You won't believe me but I genuinely tried to help him and Joan."

"Did you supply him with the drugs?"

Peter nodded. "Yes and I'm sorry now but, as I've said…"

His solicitor leaned across and put his hand on his arm as if to stop him.

"Did you know that Stella's daughter is called Christina and that she was fathered by Cezar?" Cyril looked directly at Peter, folded his arms and leaned back in his chair. "We have the DNA evidence to prove it."

Peter looked at his solicitor with a genuine look of shock and confusion. Fighting the disbelief and the growing inner anger, he collected his emotions after a few moments to ask, "How is Rose or Christina?"

Liz spoke immediately. "She's well."

Cyril wanted to pursue his thoughts on the child now that they had destabilised him. "What did you talk to Cezar about at the restaurant the other day?"

"I shouldn't have been there really. I went in to ensure that Joan and her mother were looked after but he was there. I bumped into him coming out of the toilet as I was going in. He wanted me to drop off a package, yes, before you ask, probably drugs or money for drugs, I didn't ask. He asked how Joan was and suggested he'd find out for himself. Inspector you know what he was suggesting? He was threatening. If I didn't take the package he would rape her and believe me, he would."

Cyril looked at Liz and raised an eyebrow, knowing that the historic DNA evidence against Cezar supported that possibility.

"And so, what happened?"

"I took the package. I dropped it where he'd said." He turned to his solicitor who nodded. "I dropped it in a litter bin on the Leeds Road."

"Sorry, let's get this straight. You were to drop it in a litter bin? Why couldn't he do that?"

Peter laughed. "Because he was testing me, seeing if I was still loyal, seeing if I could be trusted. He probably collected the fucking stuff himself straight afterwards, how do I know? Look, I've learned the painful way. Follow instructions, keep your head down and don't believe in fairies or angels for that matter. Believe me there is a hell on this earth because sometimes I've learned that the angels and the devil can be one and the same thing."

Cyril made a note; somehow the sentence struck a chord.

"That's the truth, the honest truth, unless you're going to get me to admit to killing Jesus Christ and then…I'm here for ever."

"What, of all this, does Joan know?"

"Nothing, simply nothing and to be honest, she's the only true and honest human being I know right now. I'd do anything, and I mean anything to protect her. Deal drugs for Cezar? Too right I will, if it keeps her safe. There'll come a time when someone will get bored with Cezar. He'll make too many mistakes and then, with luck, he'll just disappear. If that had happened sooner, then I wouldn't be here now. Drew might have straightened his life out and some people might still have their teeth and have needed fewer stitches, who knows? Life is about dealing with the now, not the what ifs. Yes, to carrying his drugs, to being afraid, to having to look over my shoulder every day, I'm guilty and I'm so sorry but, Chief Inspector, I'm still here to talk to you and if I'd refused at any time, I wouldn't be!"

"Peter Anton, you've admitted to possessing and dealing with class 'A' drugs. I've two choices considering your frank statement. I'm in a position to charge you now or you can be bailed pending further enquiries. I need to speak with my colleagues and then your solicitor."

Cyril and Liz left the room so that Peter could confer with his solicitor. He would then either be taken to the cells or released once the bail was set.

***

Cyril inhaled the menthol vapour and sipped a coffee. Liz was silent too.

"He thought Christina was his, you know that?" Liz said interrupting the silence.

Cyril nodded.

"I think I might sell my grandmother if this Cezar guy, who seems to be as evil as they come, told me to."

"You know Liz, when Cezar knows that we have Anton, he's going to do something daft. Let's put Anton out on bail and let's see if he attracts our guy."

"You can't put him in danger. You know Cezar's a total nutter and you can also probably predict the outcome."

Cyril just looked at her. "When you're between a rock and a hard place you have but one choice. And in the words of today's youth... Am I bothered?"

"What if he targets the kids?"

"My gut says not, he wants Anton."

"I'll set up a close watch on his house and at his work place, I'll liaise with Leeds," Liz instigated.

Owen walked in.

"You two look as though you've lost a fiver and found a tanner, I bring tidings of great joy! Our farmer friend has the details of the purchaser on the V5 return but it's cobblers. He said that he was with a female who drove a green van. Registration number turns out to belong to a green van owned by a guy in a place called Orrell which is..."

"Near Wigan!" Cyril interrupted. "Used to have a good rugby union team. Go on Owen, stop stating the bloody obvious!"

"He said that his son recognised the van, a Mercedes Sprinter, short wheel base. He told me that it's an unusual colour for a Sprinter as they're usually always white. Says he's seen it a few times around Greys Lane, just off Forest Lane Head."

Owen waited for Cyril to digest this information but he just looked at Owen patiently, vapour trickling out of each nostril.

"And?" Cyril asked knowing Owen was keen to continue.

"Rares Negresco had his caravan just off Forest Lane Head near to Greys Lane. That's where I first saw Cezar, said he'd stopped for a piss, the lying bastard."

"Liz, when you've organised Anton's watch, take two officers and go and check it out. Show his photo-fit to anyone in the cottages near by. Print off a picture of this type of van off the web. Make sure that it's green if you can and show that too. Get traffic to set up a patrol car on Forest Lane Head by the junction of Greys Lane and get them to stop motorists and make enquiries. The locals should have seen him or the van. I'll have back-up standing by should you need it, but to be honest, the old gut says he no longer calls at that address."

***

Sanda looked nervous. It was unusual to be brought into the office. She was alone. Angel and Hai Yau were in the kitchen. She had been told to wait. The more Angel looked at her, the more she despised him. She was more than grateful that she would not be alone in the room with him. Father and son entered.

"Sit please, Sanda. We've been discussing the help you gave us when the police called. Your quick thinking saved the day. My son seemed to freeze and be incapable of clear thought. Fortunately everyone reacted as they should have done and said nothing at all but you, Sanda, you spoke up, you were as creative in your thinking as you are in our kitchen."

Her eyes fell on Angel's and she could read his thoughts before censoring them by looking away. She felt a shudder at the thought of him in the barn.

"We must get you to learn English and then, who knows? What I do know is that you are now my second in command in the kitchen; you have been promoted to a position of trust. As I said before, it will mean more money and your own room. You already work hard and the other staff members respect you. What do you say?"

Sanda looked down and locked her hands in front of her. She lifted her head, looked at Hai Yau and smiled. "Thank you so much. I shall work hard."

"In my home town we have a saying, Sanda. It's this: *Skills can never be one's burden.* We'll give you many skills."

Hai Yau approached, lifted her to her feet and kissed her on both cheeks. "Your new job begins now. We'll go and inform the staff."

Angel stood and moved to her but she turned away. His father noticed the rebuff but he simply smiled. He spoke in English so that Sanda would not fully understand.

"If you want this one, you will have to earn her respect. She has a will and a mind of her own. Neither you nor your position frightens her. So now you must try to win back the trust you have so obviously lost, my son. Is that understood? She works for me and you will respect that privileged position by keeping these off her." He waved his hands. "Understood my son?"

Sanda looked at Angel. She could feel his resentment and inside she suddenly felt in control. She smiled at his father and went into the kitchen.

***

The large Police van filled Peter Anton's drive its darkened windows offering privacy. There was no police tape barrier but a uniformed officer stood in front of the house. Cezar could not see him from his present location but he knew that he was there. The footpath he was on stretched diagonally across the field that bordered Peter's back garden. He had stopped by the solitary oak tree and rolled a cigarette. He could see the white-suited figures in the back room.

Another was upstairs and the lights in each room were on even though it was daylight. Other temporary, more powerful lights could be seen in the background. He inhaled deeply and smiled as he wondered just how long it would take them to find it. Moving away, he turned his collar up as he climbed the stile at the base of the slope before walking to the main road. Within minutes he was driving back to the farm for the last time.

***

Owen inspected the cobbled and muddy farmyard before climbing out of the car. The pungency of the air had a density that disgusted him. He then glanced cautiously at his shoes; he suddenly realised it was not all mud that he was standing in. A dog barked, straining on the full extent of a short chain, its teeth showing in between the machine-gun bursts of barking. To his left a man appeared from a barn, his brown overalls tucked into muddy Wellington boots. He moved towards the dog taking hold of the collar and adjusted the flat tweed cap on his head. The barking ceased. Owen wondered if he were preparing to release the animal.

"Can a help thi?"

"Police, Mr Benson. I just need some information about the flat-bed you sold for scrap."

"Some folks 'av work to do."

"Tell me about it, sir. A few questions and I'm away. Suddenly I've developed an appetite, must be the aroma of the countryside."

The farmer smiled. "Come, she'll not bite thi." He released his hand from the collar and the dog settled.

"He 'ad a green van, didn't take that much notice, more interested in the brass he were givin' me. My lad'll know more. He knows about cars and stuff. I couldn't care bloody less. I'll tell thi one thing, even though it were knackered and not legal, he still buggered off in it. I told 'im he were breakin' t'law."

"Do you have security cameras in the yard, Mr Benson?"

The farmer pointed to the dog. His facial expression suggested that he was in no mood for stupid questions.

"I see," said Owen as he glanced around again briefly. He should have known better than to presume that this small piece of Yorkshire had crawled into the twenty first century.

The man's son arrived carrying a large mug of what looked like tea and handed it to his father.

"This fella wants to know more about buyer o' truck. I'll leave thi to it. Don't be long!"

"Green Merc Sprinter, battered to buggery it were too, rust everywhere. Woman drivin' it, looked a bit of a tart, wouldn't get out 'cos she'd get mucky like. Heavy make up unlike the scruffy, big bastard she brought with her."

Owen looked at the lad who appeared not to be a figure of sartorial elegance himself.

"Right. Anything else?"

"His eyes were everywhere. For a couple a days afterwards we kept a check on the farm. These 'gypo' types 'll nick owt they can see."

"Now, about the van. I believe you've seen it before."

"Mi girl lives in Knaresborough and I've seen it near Greys Lane, usually parked off the road by the trees. It's as if he's hidin' it like. Know it 'cos of the colour. Usually them vans are white and going like fuck when ya see 'em. Want a brew?"

Owen realised he'd reached the extent of the lad's knowledge and looking at the colour of his hands and nails, he declined the offer. '*Christ*', he thought, '*I'm turning into Cyril!*'

He manoeuvred the car round before stopping at the road. A Ford Focus approached. Owen waited until it had passed and then pulled out. Had he looked carefully at the driver he would have been surprised, if not a little anxious. Cezar on the other hand paid little attention to the waiting car; he just needed to get to Tanglewood Farm.

Fate is strange. Had Owen identified the driver, how different the next few days might have been.

***

"When Forensics have finished at your address, Mr Anton, you'll be released on bail pending further enquiries and subject to certain conditions. You must surrender your passport and identity card if you carry one. You must call here in person every day at a time that's convenient to your working schedule. The alternative is arrest. I imagine that you'll be able to return home this afternoon." Cyril stood. "I'll give you a few minutes to consider the situation."

***

The police vehicle moved off the drive leaving only the uniformed police officer. It had been a long shift. A lady approached with a cup of tea.

"You've been here so long, brought you a cuppa." She smiled.

PC Jones knew what was coming next and right on cue, he was not disappointed.

"What's he been up to? You can tell me, I'll not say anything."

He looked across at the three local press photographers before declining both offers from the neighbour. She turned away, emptying the cup of tea into the road and muttering under her breath.

***

Anton collected his possessions and was in the solicitor's car by three in the afternoon. It was then that he knew his real troubles had begun.

***

Cezar pressed the buttons on the pad and the gate slowly opened. He drove up the driveway parking in the yard. He had already organised his escape and it would only take minutes providing there were no interruptions.

He collected rope and tape from the barn, a small iron crowbar and a bag that he had previously secreted in the hay-loft. The small dog belonging to Mrs Yau came into the barn and yapped excitedly, running around his feet. He put down the bag and bent down extending his hand to the dog. It wagged its tail and ran excitedly towards him. It didn't see the iron bar in the other raised hand. It made no sound as its small skull was crushed. He picked up the limp carcass and hung it by its pink, diamante collar on a hook from one of the beams next to some brown sacking. It's still-moist tongue lolled from its broken face.

Nobody was in the yard. He simply loaded the car and drove away. Mrs Yau came to the door to see the taillights glow red as he slowed for the opening electric gate. She relaxed knowing it was Cezar and called for her dog.

Chapter Twenty Six

Liz turned left off Wetherby Road before driving through the ornate, gilded gates that marked the entrance to Stonefall Cemetery. The crematorium chapel was set well off the road. Cyril checked his watch. They were early. As usual, he shook it and looked again but as usual, there was no difference other than the second hand sweep.

Typically on these occasions, a light veil-like misting of rain soon drifted across the rows of gravestones that seemed to pack the grassed area to their left adding to the misery of the surroundings.

"Bloody hell, it's as if it's turned on, pre-ordered and comes with the moment, like the morbid music and the arrival of the hearse," Cyril moaned.

Liz turned her head and, as if on cue, the two black limousines crept through the gates before negotiating a small roundabout. They, in turn, were followed by only two other cars.

"It's like they're coming to the Ark, what with the increased rain!" mumbled Liz as the downpour intensified. "Joan was correct, sir. That's not many to celebrate a life lived. I hope you're in good voice!"

Cyril said nothing as he watched the coffin pass. He looked at the small presentation of flowers that was scattered across the coffin's lid, an arrangement that seemed both caring and yet haphazard. He could see Joan in the second limousine, two small heads barely visible on either side of her. He felt for her.

Liz nudged Cyril's arm and pointed to a tall figure some distance away towards the memorial garden. He was standing by a grave, umbrella in one hand and flowers in the other. Neither the rain nor the progression of incoming vehicles had distracted the solitary stranger; he simply bent and arranged the flowers by the headstone.

"Would he be so foolish, sir?"

Cyril said nothing. He looked around at the few parked vehicles, there was no green van.

"The undertakers will be outside with the cars during the service. I'll have a word for them to keep an eye on him."

On entering, the music was certainly not celebratory, it was more reflective, more melancholy. He could visualise Owen being there in place of Liz. He'd be complaining about it being downright bloody miserable and that if this was what funerals were about, then he for one definitely wasn't going to die! It brought a smile to his lips.

Joan and the two children, each holding a small posy of flowers sat at the front near the dark, gothic-style door. Five others joined the congregation but that was, for the moment, the total. Cyril and Liz moved near the back, it seemed polite to leave room for family should more arrive. Liz nudged Cyril and as Peter Anton entered, he briefly rested a hand on Joan's shoulder before moving to the row opposite Liz and Cyril. Noticing Cyril, he nodded.

Cyril's eyes did not linger. He turned his gaze taking in the chapel. The stained glass window was positioned above the coffin resting on the catafalque. He thought of Drew's body parts spread along the side of the road and wondered how they had been arranged in the box in front of him. One more person entered, soaked by the increasing incessant rain, distracting him from his bizarre thoughts.

He had hoped that Mr and Mrs Baines would have seen sense and forgotten their antipathy, if only briefly, for the sake of the children at least. Considering the time, it did not seem as though they would have the decency to attend. Cyril had registered during his brief, first encounter with Mrs Baines, that for her, tolerance and compassion were alien traits. He then caught sight of Mr Baines shaking his umbrella in the porch before entering. Cyril looked for Mrs Baines, but as he had thought, Joan's father was alone. Gregory stood and ran to him, throwing his arms around his grandfather's waist. Mr Baines bent and kissed the boy tenderly on the head before moving quickly to be with his daughter. She immediately broke down in tears

Cyril's voice, although adding to the hymn's volume, could not be classed as tuneful but to compensate, it had power. At least he sang with an unashamed enthusiasm and on this occasion, that was all that was required.

It was during the hymn that Gregory moved to leave, he was clearly too distressed by the service to stay. Mr Baines took his hand, reassuring Joan that it was all right; his younger sister seemed fine, more distracted by the flowers she was carrying than the solemnity of the service for her father. Mr Baines stopped to select his umbrella from the stand as Gregory slipped his hand and darted outside. Cyril watched and started to move but then relaxed and continued to sing as the boy's grandfather followed the child.

**

The plastic bag containing the blood-stained wallet and photographs found behind the gas fire at Peter Anton's house, was one of the items that made up the collection of incriminating evidence that was stacking up against him. Although he might carry Joan's photograph, it was unlikely that he would treasure a wedding picture and a holiday photograph of the children when they were young. The wallet had to have belonged to Drew and should that be the case, he would be brought straight back in for questioning. Peter Anton seemed adept at walking a thin high wire and so far, staying aloft.

**

At the conclusion of the service the coffin remained in place whilst the mourners left. There was no lowering of the coffin or closure of curtains and Joan was grateful for that. She walked her daughter to the coffin and lifted her so that she could place her posy on the lid. Joan put her down and placed her right hand next to the flowers. Her goodbye was said. Cyril watched Anton follow her out and he and Liz were the last to shake the vicar's hand.

The rain had stopped but the sky threatened more. He looked in the direction in which he had seen the solitary man but he, like the rain had disappeared. Cyril became aware of the slight commotion by the limousine and moved quickly to Joan's side.

"Gregory, where's Gregory?" she quizzed the undertaker who seemed a little confused as to whom she referred. "My son, the boy who travelled with us."

"He went across there with the elderly gentleman. I think they were going to the memorial garden, there's a small stream and bridge. He was trying to calm the child."

Cyril and Liz moved quickly. They ran in the general direction following the sign to the garden. There was nobody on the bridge. Cyril scanned from left to right concentrating on the trees at the boundary. There was nothing. Liz had gone to the right. He heard her call and his heart sank.

***

Stuart leaned into the incident room and spotted his quarry, Owen.

"They've found the Sprinter, parked on the car park at Rudding Park. Not suspicious. We're bringing it in after it's been checked. Anything from the house?"

Owen showed Stuart the wallet and other items they had removed for testing.

"Do you think he had a hand in Drew's death? He was there with the dogs?"

"It seems that way otherwise why would he have the wallet?" Owen responded.

"Is there any evidence that this Cezar guy has been in his house?"

"Not yet, why?"

"If he has, considering the reputation he's developing, I wouldn't put it past him to plant evidence. He's a cunning old fox. You mark my words."

Owen pointed a finger at him. "A tenner says he's never been there."

"You're on."

***

"Here, I'm down here."

Cyril could see Liz crouching in the bush. He immediately read the look in her eyes and he knew he'd underestimated the situation.

"Sorry. Liz! Got that totally wrong."

Liz said nothing but her facial expression suggested agreement.

Mr Baines was sitting with his back to the narrow trunk of a sapling, blood running from a head wound. The rainwater mixing and diluting the blood on his face made the injury look far worse than it probably was.

"It's him. He's taken Gregory. He hit him! Can you believe he's taken the child! I told that Sergeant but he obviously hasn't done anything about our concerns."

He started to weep, more out of anger than pain. "He hit him, how could a grown man do that to a child? He simply picked him up like a rag doll and carried him off."

Cyril took out his phone and dialled. Within minutes a full abduction emergency plan would be in effect and an ambulance was on its way for Mr Baines.

"Liz, get Joan and her daughter back home. There'll be additional resources waiting." As he spoke the police sirens could be heard. Cyril looked at the prints in the wet ground and started to follow what he could only hope were those left by Cezar.

***

Peter Anton banged on the kitchen door of the restaurant and the frenetic cacophony had Sanda dashing to open it. Hai Yau stood confused by the intrusion. Peter burst in.

"He's taken a child, he said he would. He told me that if Sadler's family went to the police he'd harm the kids. Jesus, he's going to do something stupid," he ranted in English.

Sanda went and poured a brandy and handed it to him as Angel came in.

"Who?" Hai Yau demanded.

Angel answered for Peter. "Bloody Cezar. I've just taken a call from my mama, she saw him. He's cleared his stuff from the farm and," he paused looking at his father, "he's killed mother's dog." He put his hand to his lips. "Why would he do that? Mother was always so kind to him, always. Why is he involved with the Sadler family? Why would they go to the police?"

"He made them pay for drugs that their son-in-law had been given and had failed to pay for. The fact that we killed the man accidentally in the tunnel had no effect on Cezar, a debt is a debt which has to be paid."

"We'll never know, my son, but these things are done for a reason. We now know he no longer belongs in our family and that he's given us a sign. In some ways he's not been settled since we started this restaurant. He thinks we're moving away from the world that was our foundation. He believes we're selling our past for a future that moves from the unlawful to the lawful, from the dark into the light. He's frightened that he has none of the skills our new world needs and he's afraid. Yet, I know, that we can survive in both worlds and that one will support the other. Go home and comfort your mother. Peter and I have plans to make, we've a pebble to toss into a pond; we'll do nothing rash as that's what he wants."

Sanda moved out of the kitchen and onto the car park. She inhaled the fresh air. Angel came out and looked at her. She moved to his car.

"What's happening? I understand nothing, but I sense trouble with Cezar."

"You're simply a cook and that's what you do. My father thinks you're wonderful but you show me little respect. Maybe if you were to understand English and be a little more welcoming, we might get on but for now, you're nothing."

The car moved away and Sanda was alone. A police car flashed past down Otley Road, its siren off but with the blue strobe lights flashing. She walked out of the car park and away from the restaurant.

***

The footprints led Cyril to the edge of a children's playground and a small housing estate before disappearing. Cyril assumed correctly that Cezar had left his car near the site and carried the child to the vehicle. Nobody would have suspected abduction, but with the rain, there was nobody about to see him. He could now be anywhere. Cyril made his way back to Liz's car. Thankfully she had left the keys with a groundsman.

"Lady said you wouldn't be long and you'd need these." He smiled. Another hearse approached. Cyril sat in the car with his head in his hands. How could he have been so bloody naïve?

***

Sanda stopped at the security box and an officer looked at her apron and small black chef's hat.

"I need to speak with Detective Chief Inspector Bennett, I believe a child has been taken and I can help." Sanda's English was not perfect but neither was it non existent as she had made out.

The Officer picked up the phone. There was a pause. He raised his eyebrows. "I'm sorry, he's busy. Can I take a message?"

"Please call his mobile, he can't contact me and he must speak with me now."

Cyril's mobile rang. "Bennett."

"Sir, I've a young lady at the gate. Sanda is her name. She tells me that you know her and that she has information concerning the abducted child. Says she might be able to help. Do you want me to fire her off and come back later?"

"Put her on."

The officer handed her the phone and she leaned into the open security office window.

"Inspector Bennett. Can we meet now I need to talk to you? When we do, I'll no longer be able to return to the restaurant, I'll be finished."

"I thought your English didn't exist?"

"I realised that by seeing and hearing and saying nothing, I learned more, giving me a special weapon. I need to use that weapon now for the sake of this missing child."

"Put the police officer back on, Sanda, please."

"Allocate a WPC to be with her at all times. Put her in my office and don't let her leave. I'll be there in ten minutes."

***

Sanda sat looking at Cyril's orderly desk. She stood to look at a small, framed cartoon that was on the wall. It showed a large policeman with a huge bushy moustache peering through a hole in a wooden fence trying to watch a football match. A child was placing a firecracker behind him. She smiled. It was then that she noticed Cyril.

"You're an anomaly, young lady. One day you understand nothing and here you are fully conversant in the Queen's English. It must have been very useful listening to conversations you shouldn't have been privy to, valuable too?"

Sanda smiled. "I kept it for a rainy day I think you say. Right now, Inspector Bennett, there is a very dark sky indeed and although I'm safe and free from guilt, I'm frightened for the child. I know Cezar well and I know just what he's capable of."

"How well do you know him?"

"Too well, I am ashamed to say, he's my father."

Cyril nearly choked. "Your father?"

"Nobody at the restaurant knows. I hadn't seen him since he left my mom, we knew that he had come to England but he never sent money or wrote. The last we heard was that he was in Leeds. I was young when he had to leave Romania, he's wanted by the police for drugs offences, running prostitutes, gambling and violence. You've seen him work. When we were allowed to travel here I grabbed the opportunity. I arrived in England and I decided to go to Leeds. Believe me, it wasn't what I expected. I thought that I would walk into a job, I would be given a house and money for things but...you hear so many lies back home from people who are here. I began to sleep rough. It was then that I decided to speak only Romanian so that I would know my own and be safe. Fellow Romanians helped me; they gave me work and a place to stay. Things changed, they took my passport, fed me but refused to pay me.

I realised what they wanted me for. I tried to leave but I was raped. It was then that I saw him. He came to look at me, to see if I would do. At first, I didn't recognise my father, he looked different, his missing teeth and his nose maybe. He didn't recognise me either, but why should he? I was just another silly girl who was going to become a potential whore. He seemed taller than I remembered and much older. I saw his face change when I mentioned my name and my village. He asked me what my father's name was and then my mother's. When I replied, he almost crumbled. I was then reminded of his violent side. He left the room and I heard him ask the men what I was like for sex. One of the men bragged immediately. The man didn't speak again. I don't know what happened to him but my father had blood on his hand when he reappeared."

"And so the story you told us when we were at the restaurant wasn't true, you were simply protecting him?"

"I was protecting Hai Yau. Nobody else ever really cared other than Rares. He's been like a father to me. He's kind and considerate, unlike his son."

"So how did you become involved with Hai Yau and the restaurant?"

"My father worked for him, they have many criminal activities hidden within the seemingly innocent food trade. These hidden parts are what my father knows well and therefore helps run and organise; prostitution, gambling, dogs, drugs and people. I suppose it's known as slavery. They ensure that people work for very little, usually they are the illegal migrants who are frightened of being sent home, frightened of the police but more frightened of my father. These are the easiest to control and dispose of, after all who knows they are even here? It's easy to move people Inspector, too easy."

"So why now, Sanda?"

"When Peter Anton came to the kitchen today he was scared, very scared, but it wasn't for himself, but for the child. When I heard that my father had taken a child I had to come. Inspector, Romanian fathers don't spare the rod. I still have marks on my body from beatings I suffered when I was very little. He will stop at nothing. If he's made a promise or a threat, then I know he will carry it out. When I was living at the farm, Angel raped me. I dared not tell my father. Angel, I believe, told Cezar that a boy called Rares had raped me. He would tell everyone, but in fact, Rares was kind to me when it happened and I believe Angel was jealous. Rares seems to have disappeared and I haven't seen him since I left the farm. Peter told Hai Yau that Cezar threatened a family if they spoke to the police. Sorry, I must be confusing you with my poor English!"

"So where is he?"

"I don't know but maybe he will stop if I ask him to, I don't know, I just want in some way to stop this mess."

Owen didn't knock he just burst into the room, the WPC jumped and turned.

"He's been spotted! No sign of the child as yet."

Owen rushed around the desk, went to the computer and brought up Google maps onto the screen. The satellite image detailing the area around Follifoot was clear.

"Liz said that he's probably gone to ground and I immediately thought of the Brunswick Tunnel, but then why would he go back there? Someone's just telephoned to say that they'd seen our suspect near the disused Prospect Tunnel, it's an old tunnel that's within walking distance of Peter's house. It seemed logical. Look!"

Owen showed the approximate entrance of the tunnel and the pathways along the disused track.

"Beeching has a lot to answer for, Owen," Cyril commented but immediately could see from the look on Owen's face that he did not have the faintest idea what he was talking about.

"He's had plenty of time to plan for such a situation and the bastard's run from the police before and escaped. All he has to do is lie low."

"There's a reason for all of this. He can't hope to get money for the safe release of the boy and he doesn't want the burden of the child if he plans to run. He's drawing someone in."

Cyril looked carefully at the image on the screen. Can we get details and photographs of the tunnel?"

"There are several but why pick this place? If he's in there, he's trapped. Close both ends with coppers and dogs and he's going nowhere."

"Mark my words, Sir, if he's in there, then there's a definite reason but I'm buggered if I know what his game is."

"Sanda, I want you to remain here, you'll be well cared for and safe but I might need your further help later. Is that alright?"

She nodded and the WPC took her away. She stopped and turned to Cyril. "Don't let him harm the child, no matter what, promise me that."

Cyril said nothing. He was not in a position to know his next move let alone make promises that might be impossible to keep. Besides the boy might already be dead.

Chapter Twenty Seven

Cyril was determined to get a confirmed sighting before he ordered in an armed unit and intensive search team. Two dogs were organised, one to search the ground above the tunnel and check the woodland that surrounded the three blanked tunnel air vents that were now probably concealed in the undergrowth, whilst the other dog and handler would enter to check the tunnel moving from the northerly portal. Officers would be positioned at the southerly portal, the only exit.

The tunnel ran for about a thousand yards before the empty, trackless route led to the used line that still carried trains from Leeds to Harrogate. It turned sharply and ran over the thirty-one arched Crimple Valley Viaduct. Cyril sat with Owen and looked at the satellite image of the site and traced the route with his finger.

"There appears to be a house built on the old line preventing entry onto the track and the viaduct. That will need checking. We need to be ready to move together. I want everyone in position in two hours. No lights 'n sounds. I neither want him panicked nor forewarned if he's there. Liaise with British Transport Police, we need the viaduct checked and officers positioned at the junction between the disused line and the live line."

***

Cyril checked his watch, all was ready. There had been no further sightings but the tunnel had to be checked. As planned, the dogs and officers combed the woodland that ran over the tunnel but there was nothing. The three air vents were still capped and showed no signs of interference. The second group followed the German Shepherd as it ploughed through the saturated, muddy tunnel, also to no avail. There was nothing from the Transport Police either; the viaduct was clear.

"Where the bloody hell are you, you bastard?" Cyril asked himself. He stood in the entrance to the southerly portal. The wind tunnelling through was chill and he stared at the glow of light at the far end. If only he could see light at the end of his endeavour he would be a happy man.

"Let's hope he's not watching us from some safe place laughing at our clumsy efforts. He's certainly caused us to waste man power and time," Owen said angrily. They both turned through three hundred and sixty degrees to see if there was an obvious vantage point. There was none.

Cyril put a call out. "I want two cars to Tanglewood Farm, off Tang Lane. Have back up close by, two other cars to the Zingaro restaurant. Get them to remain visible until further notice if our man is not found. That will make two fewer places he can go."

***

Cezar moved through the farmyard carrying the large sack. The dog that had an hour ago strained at the full extent of the chain lay curled, its paws in the air, its legs bent. Blood had splashed the cobbles and soaked into the mud and straw but the large gash along its throat was crusted and home to feasting flies. The yard was now quiet. He opened the boot of the newly requisitioned Subaru Outback estate car and loaded the bag. He returned for the length of rope and torches. He noticed that there was a slight movement from inside the sack but it soon subsided. He had parked his Focus out of sight in the barn behind a rather large green tractor. He walked back into the farmhouse.

"You spoke with the police; I hate the fucking police and now I hate you." He checked the electrical ties that bound their hands and legs. The knotted gags blocked their mouths. The younger man's limp body was curled in a foetal position, his legs beneath the large table; he had taken a severe beating but he was lucky to be still breathing. The older man had been hit once. Cezar could still detect defiance in his eyes and slapped him again.

"Look at me again like that you old bastard and I'll blow your fucking brains across this poxy room."

On the table lay a shotgun, some cartridges and a mobile phone that he'd taken from the son. He picked up the youth's mobile phone and slipped it in his pocket.

"He'll not be needing it for a while and I'll return the car." His smile suggested that he lied. He spit on the floor.

He checked the shotgun and put a cartridge in each barrel before walking over to the old man. He placed the barrel to his head.

"Bang!" Cezar shouted. The old man simply fainted.

Cezar was still laughing as he closed and locked the door. He tossed the keys towards the dead dog before climbing into the car.

***

Cyril sat in the incident room, he neither drank the coffee that had been placed in front of him nor touched his electronic cigarette. He was deep in thought. There was no sign of Cezar at the Baines' house but then why should there be? He was absent from Hai Yau's farm, although he had been there and the dog that had been removed from the hook in the barn told of Cezar's mental state. He had not been seen at the restaurant. There was enough evidence to arrest Hai Yau and his son for many crimes including employment of people in the shady and sinister black economy, but at this moment Cyril was better where he was, the arrests could wait. As long as they were free there was a chance that Cezar would make some kind of contact.

Cyril felt impotent. He had placed so many of his chess pieces in vulnerable positions that he wondered if he had scared Cezar from making the next move. Until he had a lead, another sighting or until Cezar responded, he could go nowhere. He checked his watch; it had been five and a half hours since the child had gone missing. The incident room was manned to capacity and the photographs of Gregory had gone nationwide on radio, television and the Internet. All leads were being followed but there was nothing concrete. Cyril inhaled but took no satisfaction from the vapour.

***

Cezar turned off Hookstone Road and onto the twin roads that led to and from the industrial estate. He drove to the far end and parked away from the cameras. He checked the full extent of the car park thoroughly searching for occupied vehicles or pedestrians before climbing out of the car. He then walked to the footpath hugging the car park edge which meandered, half-hidden by foliage, to the footbridge that ran over the railway. His position on the bridge allowed Cezar to check the line; it was quiet. He returned to the car and retrieved the sack and the rope before heading back to the bridge. The dead weight of the child made climbing the wall and travelling down the steep banking difficult, but he managed. Once on the trackside he rested, sweat beading his forehead. He took a deep breath and lifted the sack before heading towards the viaduct. Checking his watch before moving he concealed himself in the overgrown banking. He had planned well.

***

Owen tapped the white board before turning to Cyril.

"What if, sir, he always seeks revenge? People talking to the police whether they instigate it or not seem to make him insanely angry. I've got a strange feeling, could he be holed up at Benson's farm, the guy he bought the flatbed from? The son said he had eyes all over. Was he checking it out for a possible bolt hole?"

"Call him now!" Cyril stood. A flutter of nerves hit his stomach as he eagerly watched Owen who simply shook his head.

"The line's dead."

"Get one of the cars from Tanglewood Farm to take a look, they're nearby."

***

Cezar watched the two carriages of the Leeds bound train pass him. It was on time. It travelled slowly across the viaduct before finally turning sharp right and disappearing out of view. In five minutes the train bound for Harrogate and then York would pass the other way. This train would pass only feet away from him. He would then have just over the hour before the penultimate evening service would trundle by. Not exactly like clockwork, the train rounded the bend before heading over the viaduct, its two-tone horn sounding its approach. It was soon visible and heading towards Hornbeam Park Station. He lifted the boy's drugged body held inside the nylon builder's rubble sack and moved towards the centre arch of the viaduct.

It was nearly dark but he had enough light to work by. The beams of the moving cars way below to his left could be seen moving snake-like along the road. The wind was stronger than earlier and he felt its chill. He stopped to listen. He heard only the wind and the screech of a distant owl. Carefully tying the rope to the handles, he checked the knot before positioning the bundle next to the parapet. He threaded the rope under the first metal railway track and crossed to the second. He dug away the chippings to allow the rope to be looped round the metal before tying it off around one of the concrete sleepers. Moving back to the bag, he held the rope, checking the strength of both knots. He wanted neither to become loose prematurely. Once satisfied, he lifted the bag before lowering it over the edge until, once free of the masonry, it began to swing. The rope was taut, at full stretch, hanging in the centre of the arch. He looked at his watch, he would have an hour before the penultimate Harrogate bound train would pass this point, its wheels acting as a natural executioner. He rolled a cigarette, inhaled and spat onto the line. The stretched rope creaked as the breeze increased the pendular action of the dangling bag. He had one more task to complete and he was done, finished. He smiled.

He took the mobile phone from his pocket and dialled the Baines' house. Joan answered tentatively.

"Put the old, miserable fucking battle-axe of a bitch on now or you'll never hear from me again or discover the whereabouts of your son for that matter."

The officers listened in, the conversation relayed live to the incident room.

Barbara Baines came to the phone, she was tearful and her bravado had gone. "Please bring him home, please. I didn't know that Reg had gone to the police, please, I beg you."

"Listen, remember what you said you would do if I took one of the kids? Remember you evil old witch? You said I'd hang." He paused, giving her time to digest his words and hear the sound of his breath. "Wrong! But he is, your little boy. In fact he's hanging right now but not for much longer. They won't catch me and I doubt they'll even find him in a hurry. He's not dead but very soon the executioner's blade will fall and ..." he laughed and didn't finish the sentence. He hung up.

Barbara heard his laughter and then nothing.

Reg walked to her and put his arms around her, Joan just crumpled on the settee.

***

The police car pulled into the farmyard, the vehicle's lights illuminating the sleeping dog. PC Blackmore stepped out and approached. He called but the dog did not move. He shone his torch and saw the blood and the mass of movement crawling and buzzing around the dog's neck.

"Patch me through to DCI Bennett immediately!"

He could instantly be heard in the incident room.

"The dog's had its throat cut and there's no sign of anyone, no lights in the farmhouse..." He then stood on the keys. "A minute!"

He waved for his colleague. Picking up the keys he approached the farmhouse, relaying the information as they progressed. The people in the incident room could hear the key in the lock and the officers entering.

"What do you see?" The voice of the controlling officer sounded urgent.

"Two victims, Sir, both bound. One has suffered a good deal of facial damage..." There was a pause. "He's still breathing."

An officer in the incident room addressed Cyril. "The caller to the Baines' house used a phone belonging to a Ray Benson, it's registered to that address." She put a written address in from of him.

"The older man is alive too, he's conscious. Says it was the guy who collected the scrap truck. He's taken a shotgun and a couple of dozen cartridges. He's driving a silver Subaru Outback estate. Call for an ambulance, it's urgent, the air ambulance if it can still fly this late."

Someone in the incident room immediately put the call out for medical assistance, to traffic and to those monitoring the town's CCTV giving the vehicle's description and the registration number.

"Sir, the old man is mumbling something about arches and hanging the bastard. Says the guy said that he was going to show that bloody family, that they'd cry when they found out that the boy was the one who was hanging and not him. He sounds very confused, probably the blow to the head."

Cyril banged his fist on the desk, his frustration beginning to show. "Shit! He's at Crimple Valley Viaduct. He was checking it out earlier, not hiding there. Get in touch with the Transport Police, check the timetable and find out train times. Call for a car to search the industrial estate at Hornbeam Park. I want an armed response unit there too, tell everyone that the suspect is armed and should be approached with extreme caution. I want no dead heroes and I want safe access to the railway line."

"Sir, next train's due in twenty-five minutes. Harrogate bound followed by Leeds bound in thirty."

"I want both trains halted at the stations before the viaduct. I say again, halted. Get confirmation immediately. I want nothing to cross that viaduct. Owen, get Sanda and the WPC 'whatever her name is', they're with us. We're going in through the garden of the house built on the old track, that's the closest to the viaduct. It's times like this that we need our own helicopter."

Cyril and Owen collected their integrated radios, adding the earpiece and microphone. They needed to stay in contact with the incident room and the officers tracking Cezar. They then collected two weapons, which despite the urgency still couldn't be rushed and had to be signed for; there never seemed to be any rush where firearms were concerned.

***

Cezar sat in the reclined driver's seat, a whisky bottle between his thighs, the barrel of the gun resting on the frame of the open driver's window. The car park was well lit. He saw the police car as it crawled down the main central road of the industrial estate. He could see it stop as the occupants scanned the car parks. Progressing slowly, it reached the car park where the Subaru sat in the far corner. It turned in. The lights shone on the car.

"That's the one that we want, Subaru estate, right colour, right registration. One man, I think, in the driver's seat." The officer looked at his partner and smiled. "Bingo!"

They saw the muzzle flash first and then the shot peppered the windscreen producing myriad cracks and chips. Fortunately it remained intact.

"Fucking hell! Back up! Back up!" the passenger yelled, his elation swiftly converting to sheer panic.

The driver slipped into reverse and swung the car at great speed. The Subaru moved forward like a stalking creature, no lights, just moving towards the stationary car.

"For Christ sake go!" The officer facing the oncoming car screamed at the driver to put his foot down as the imploding side windows followed the second flash; both officers received face and neck wounds but the police car moved quickly down the road, its blue lights now flashing and fortunately still working. As they headed to the exit a large police van turned in towards them as the Subaru began to move slowly up to them, unrushed and seemingly un-phased, its prey in its sights.

The passenger in the patrol car called in. "Silver Subaru on the car park of Hornbeam Park. Firearm discharged, I say again, firearm discharged. Firearm unit on site."

Cyril heard the call as his car, as planned, approached the solitary house built on the disused line. His driver stopped in the driveway, as did the two other vehicles. As Cyril left the car the house security lights came on and the front door opened.

"It's the Police, there's nothing to worry about!" Cyril called confidently as he marched up to the elderly occupant. "DCI Bennett, we need to get to the viaduct."

The man walked down the steps and directed them to a gate in the far boundary fence.

"Were you here earlier? My wife was mumbling about seeing somebody but, she sees many people, it's the Alzheimer's, sadly."

Cyril just nodded, he had neither time nor patience for explanations but he had an idea who it might have been.

They moved through the garden.

"Approaching the viaduct now. Is the gunman still with you?"

"Affirmative, car's come to a halt. Firearms' officers deployed."

"Make calls to all the offices on site and the hotel to keep people inside and away from windows."

"Done it, Sir."

Cyril and Owen donned head torches; having both hands free was an advantage as they moved across the uneven ground.

"Why is it I always think of Daleks when I see people wearing these?" Cyril commented, attempting to control the butterflies that had suddenly erupted in his stomach. In such situations he always felt like this, a cocktail of nerves, excitement and adrenaline. It somehow made the hours of paperwork bearable.

"Misspent youth, sir! I'll always think of that poor bastard in the tunnel. Are you OK, sir?"

Cyril simply smiled. "Never felt better, Owen. Never better."

They checked their weapons.

They cautiously left the dark of the disused cutting behind then tentatively crossed the railway tracks that shone silver, straight in the torchlight. As they ran over the viaduct, Cyril found walking along the sleepers to be the easiest route. Owen took one track and Cyril the other. They walked slowly. The other officers stopped at strategic places on either side of the track just in case there was some kind of trap or ambush. As Owen approached the centre of the viaduct he paused. He moved his head in order to focus the beam of light onto what had brought him to a halt. He was the first to see the rope in the torchlight but was unsure as to its significance.

"Just a sec, Sir. There's something across this track. Is there across yours? It's about fifteen metres ahead. Sir, looks like rope running round the track and under here and there, look! It goes over the parapet." He moved his head allowing the beam of light to follow the blue rope.

They both approached the parapet with a degree of caution and Owen leaned over first. When it was safe, Cyril followed bracing his body against the rough stone. The wind blew their hair and Cyril's eyes watered. The rope seemed to disappear under the arch and then the torchlight picked out the large bag as it swung into view. They watched as the pendulum swung the bag in and out of sight. It appeared and disappeared under the arch. The cattle grazing in the field way below seemed strange illuminated by the dispersed beams.

"He's in the bag! The boy's in the bag! The next train on this line would have severed the rope and the boy would be a mangled mess on the valley floor, all over red rover!" Owen summed up the plot perfectly if not a little too graphically.

Cyril grabbed the rope and Owen helped. "Steady, we don't want him to bang into the edge of the stone arch. Try to control the swing slowly by drawing the bag nearer to the stonework. Easy, he's coming."

Once the bag was resting against the masonry, the task was easier. The wind tried to move the bag sideways but the rough stone façade formed a brake. Owen reached over as far down as possible, grabbing the two webbing handles before hauling the sack over the parapet and placing it carefully onto the sleepers. Owen looked at Cyril. There was no movement from the bag. Neither movement nor sound. Both men inhaled.

***

There was no movement from the Subaru, or none that the police could discern apart from a wisp of grey exhaust smoke that drifted tail-like. Cezar picked up the bottle, put it to his lips and finished the contents before tossing it out of the window. It smashed on the road some distance away distracting the observers. Cezar swiftly selected reverse and sped back up the lane throwing the car into a left turn. He flicked open the door, crouched and ran to the path before turning towards the footbridge. It was dark on the pathway, all the light was now behind him. The police dog handler saw his silhouette against the backdrop. He saw the weapon held low and instantly released the dog before the man had time to react. Cezar didn't even focus on the running dog until the yellowy glow of the car park lights reflected its eyes, by which time he could neither turn the gun nor turn to run. The dog hit him hard, knocking the gun clear as its ferocious bite struck Cezar, its jaws breaking his right arm just below the elbow. He cried instinctively with the pain. With his left hand he tried to retrieve the knife that was tucked inside his coat but his attempt proved fruitless. Two armed officers aimed their weapons.

"Police! Stay down! Stay down! Still, stay still!"

The dog continued to nip and pull at Cezar's only defensive arm. Blood from the hand wounds glowed shiny wet in the powerful torch beams that were attached to the police firearms. The handler recalled his dog. Reluctantly, but obediently Luger backed off, rarely taking its eyes from the downed suspect until securely held by his handler. The dog barked twice and was then silent as it was taken further away from the prostrate figure. The handler was ready to release the dog again should it be needed. Cezar turned and looked at both men and then at the dog but said nothing, he simply groaned as he lifted his broken right arm after one of the officers instructed him to move his arms away from his body.

***

Cyril untied the ropes and opened the bag cautiously. Wrapped in the nylon shroud was the boy. He tentatively leaned in, searching for the boy's neck to check for a pulse. He smiled and nodded to Owen.

"He's alive." As he spoke the boy vomited, the hot, sticky fluid flooded all over Cyril's arm and hand.

"Shit!"

"Actually no, sir." Owen could only smile. "It's the drugs and motion sickness from the pendulum swing that have combined into that heady cocktail we fondly know as vomit," Owen couldn't resist saying, as he knew just how much this would affect Cyril. Bodily fluids and Cyril did not mix well. Cyril's complexion now seemed even more pallid in the torch light and his facial expression mirrored his disgust.

"Man apprehended, confirm that he's our suspect. No police injuries," they both heard over the radio.

"Boy's safe but a little unwell. Ambulance needed at meeting point. Any injuries to the suspect?" Cyril enquired.

"Police dog apprehended our man. He has severe dog bites and a broken right arm. Dog obviously took a fancy to him!" came the reply.

"Oh! How appropriate," said Cyril, "how bloody appropriate!" Both men laughed. "Divine retribution, Owen! Maybe Satan doesn't look after his own after all."

Owen looked skyward, the torch beam shining like a beacon.

"Dreadful smell, vomit, wouldn't you agree, sir?"

"Just pick up the boy, Owen."

"I'll carry him in the bag, sir. Safer that way."

Chapter Twenty Eight

Hai Yau, his wife and Angel cut sad figures as each sat in their own interview room, the only distraught one amongst them being Mrs Yau, who, quite frankly, seemed totally confused by the whole situation. Peter Anton was back in Interview Room Four, his foot bouncing under the table and his fingers looking as though he were playing a tune on the table.

"Modern day slavery, employing people in the black economy, trafficking in illegal immigrants, prostitution, drug running, protection and, well… the list is endless. I daren't think how long they'll get for this lot. Fancy a bet, Owen, if you've any clean fivers?"

"Oh aye! Why not? There's one good thing, we'll not be seeing Cezar for a long while. And Anton?"

"Irregular accounting, drug dealing and he's admitted to being, in his words, forced to be present at Rares Negrescu's murder. I don't think Joan will find him such a suitable catch now. She'll be damned annoyed that her mother was right after all!"

"What of Sanda?"

"Clean, nothing on her at all. Her only crime was thinking that the streets of Leeds and Harrogate were paved with free hand outs and welfare. Just hope she finds what she's looking for."

"Don't you need a housekeeper, sir?"

Cyril glared at Owen before his mobile rang. To his relief it was Dr Julie Pritchett.

"Saved by the bell, Owen, saved by the bell." There was a short conversation and Cyril smirked. "I think I'm busy this evening after we've got through some of this, Owen." He pointed to the interview rooms. "You'll just have to buy me that pint tomorrow. I seem to have a more attractive engagement." He winked and smiled at Owen.

Stuart walked past and put out a hand towards Owen who grunted and dipped into his back pocket before producing a ten-pound note. Stuart grinned. "I love DNA, don't you, sir?" He did not wait for the riposte.

Cyril looked at Owen, inhaled his menthol vapour but said nothing for a moment.

"There are winners and losers, Owen. Such is life. Gambling is a slippery slope to ruin. You of all people should know that and if not ask him in there!"

They both looked into the Interview Room at the lonely, broken figure of Peter Anton and Cyril smiled briefly. Now the real work would begin.

"Owen?"

"Sir?"

"Thanks for everything!"

He patted Owen on the shoulder, tucked his electronic cigarette into his top pocket and entered Interview Room Four.

THE END

Acknowledgements

To Debbie
What a star you are. Thank You. X
To Carrie
Thank you so much for your continued patience and support.
To Betsy and Fred of Bloodhound Books.
I'm grateful for your having faith in the Harrogate crime series
and in me. Your team has been absolutely brilliant, a huge
thanks to all concerned.

To Caroline Vincent.
A special thank you.
To Charlie and Sheila
Your support is appreciated.

Letter from Malcolm

I should firstly like to thank you for reading 'Hell's Gate'. I really hope you enjoyed the second outing of DCI Cyril Bennett and DS David Owen. They have become part of my family and although they may not seem to you to be the best police officers in the world, they are certainly keen to solve the crime, so much so, they are working on another case as you read this!

If you did enjoy it, I should be grateful if you would write a review. It is a great help to read just what you think. It might also lead other readers to discover my books for the first time. It would also be wonderful if you could recommend my books to family and friends.

This next case for Bennett and Owen awaits.

Malcolm

If you would like further details then you can always find me on:

Facebook.com/Malcolm Hollingdrake@ AuthorMalcolmHollingdrake/

Twitter Malcolm Hollingdrake@MHollingdrake